The Haunted Mirror

by

Maureen Boleyn

Published by Boleyn House
Paignton,
Devon

First published by Boleyn House 31/3/2011

ISBN 978 0 9568337 0 9

About the Author

Maureen was born in Hitchin, Hertfordshire where she met her husband, Richard, when she was only nine years old. They married a week after her eighteenth birthday and they have now been married nearly 56 years.

With 4 children, 13 grandchildren and 2 great granddaughters she leads a very full and fun-packed life living on the South Devon coast. Here they ran a small hotel but now just have family and friends to stay.

Before writing her first novel, The Silken Web, they had numerous businesses including a newsagency, soft furnishings, tea room, costume hire and a small-holding so life has never been dull.

Hitchin holds many happy memories for them. Maureen attended Hitchin Grammar School and both she and Richard were active members of the Youth Club. They married at St. Mary's Church and 2 of their children were born in the house featured in the story.

The story is fiction but the house is true.

Dedication

I would like to dedicate this book to Richard, my husband, for his patience and understanding and to all my family and friends who have encouraged me. They are too many to mention without leaving some-one out. I will just mention my daughter, Kerry, who always has faith in me and is on the other end of the phone when I need her..

I also wish to mention the house where this story takes place. It holds twenty years of happy memories for me and will always hold a special place in my heart. It is still there.

Prologue

July 1963

The room was poorly lit and the air warm and suffocating. No window had been open to relieve the oppression that was tangible.

As the old lady lay, clutching at her chest and fighting for breath, the person who was responsible watched her without offering help. She was blinking rapidly and, as his eyes met hers, his lips curled into a cruel smile. Eventually she gave up the fight and lay still. He felt nothing but a cold sensation running down his spine.

He thought himself extremely clever for he had killed the old lady without laying a finger on her. He could never be blamed or held responsible. He was in the clear and everything would be his; everything he'd worked and planned for. Perhaps worked was the wrong word for he had done nothing of any significance. He had schemed - that was all. Now all he had to do was find what he was looking for and, with the old lady out of the way, that would be easy.

There was no compassion in this man. No conscience to tug at his heart strings. It was questionable whether he had a heart. His aims were cold and calculating. He stood and waited for a few more moments, his hands clasped in tight fists at his sides, and then, taking her tiny wrist in his large, podgy fingers, felt for her pulse - there was nothing. The only thing left to do was telephone the doctor and say he had found her unconscious.

The bedcovers had become rumpled in her last struggling moments so these he straightened to give the impression that she had died peacefully in her sleep. He smiled again. It had all been so easy.

He stood for a few moments looking at her and when, at last, he turned to leave the room he caught sight of the cheval mirror standing a few feet away and suddenly caught the reflection.

Letting out an involuntary gasp he felt the hairs on his head stand on end and cold spread over him as though he had stepped into an ice-cold shower. The mirror showed his grandmother sitting up in bed - a smile playing on her lips. He turned back to the bed and there she lay - perfectly still - as still as death. Turning to the dressing table and picking up the nearest thing to hand, which happened to be a coloured glass perfume bottle, he hurled it at the mirror expecting it to shatter. At the sound of breaking glass he quickly turned away and closed his eyes but when he re-opened them and looked back, he could not believe what he was seeing. He had expected to see the mirror in pieces but it was still intact. Not only that, the reflection still showed his grandmother sitting up in bed. It was the perfume bottle that lay in fragments on the floor at his feet. - and still the reflection that stared back at him was of his grandmother smiling. He didn't stop to pick up the pieces of glass but fled from the room averting his eyes from the mirror.

By the time he had run up the next flight of stairs he was gasping for breath. It came to him that he really must try to lose some weight. He paused and panted then went to the linen cupboard and, snatching a folded sheet from the shelf, ran back down the stairs into the bedroom thrusting the sheet over the mirror. There was no breeze in the room, no window open, but as he turned to go out of the door the sheet moved as though someone was shaking it.

He made his way down to the lounge and poured himself a double whiskey. His hands were trembling and some of the contents spilled onto the red carpet. He lowered himself into a chair and put his head back against the leather. He was finding it difficult to breath but as the whiskey warmed him he began to relax. Of course he must have imagined it, he chided himself. His grandmother was dead.

It took three days for him to summon up the courage to re-enter that room. The body had been moved to the undertakers and the room was eerily quiet, the bed unmade and turned back as though his grandmother had just got up to go about her daily routine. His heart was thumping against his ribs. Grasping the mirror with two hands he lifted it with difficulty. It was heavier then he expected. Every two or three stairs he had to lower it to stop and get his breath.

Finally he reached the box room at the top of the house. It was a long L shaped room which housed old bits of discarded furniture and boxes containing old memorabilia from the past. He clambered, with difficulty, carrying the mirror around the assortment of chests and chairs before reaching the part of the room that was hidden from view round the corner. Here he placed the mirror as far away from the door as possible. As he turned to leave the room he did not notice the sheet move. He did hear the sigh that permeated the air.

You may think you have hidden me, but I have seen and I will tell. You cannot hide me. One day I will tell.

1

October 1963

In a tiny flat, in the East End of London, three months after the death of Ellen Bancroft, Sally Westwood sat at the breakfast table in her kitchen savouring a leisurely cup of coffee. She had just finished her toast and marmalade and was enjoying just sitting staring into space and listening to the radio.

Because she had stood in for another assistant and worked a couple of hours extra yesterday she did not have to be at work until ten this morning which was a rare treat. It was a bright October morning and the sun was streaming in through the window showing dust motes shivering in its rays. There was no central heating in the flat and a small paraffin stove gave the only warmth. It had taken her a while to get used to the smell but now she barely noticed it.

The house had once been, like many others in the road, a handsome dwelling that had been home to a rich trader and his family, but was now converted into small flats. Gone were the impressive high ceilings with fancy coving above rich wall coverings and in their place were the ugly, discoloured suspended ceilings hiding all the opulence of a bygone age.

Joe and Sally's flat was on the first floor and would have once been a luxurious bedroom and dressing room. Sally had often sat and tried to imagine what it would have looked like in bygones days. History had always been her favourite subject at school and she loved anything to do with the past. She dreamed of ripping off all the horrible modern plasterboard in the rooms and discovering what lay beneath. It was such a shame that these beautiful houses had to end up like this.

The sound of the letter box rattling brought her out of her reverie and told her the postman had climbed the stairs so she left the table to walk through to the hallway with a little thrill of excitement. It was strange how she always got a nice feeling when the postman called. Not that she ever received anything of interest but the feeling went way back to when she was a child. There was something nice about a postman.

Her eye caught the sight of just one envelope lying on the mat and she bent to pick it up. It was of thick, cream vellum which, to her, looked rather expensive. She turned it over in her hand and felt the sumptuous paper. The address was beautifully written in old fashioned slanted handwriting. When she saw it was addressed to her she was surprised as most post that came was for both her and Joe. She turned it over in her hand not knowing what she expected to find, but nothing was written on the back. She was both excited and reluctant to open it although she was dying to look inside. Even though it was hand written it somehow still looked official. For some unknown reason she could not give, she had always been wary of official looking envelopes. Perhaps she should wait until Joe came home before she opened it. Then she realised how foolish she was being and, anyway, she definitely could not wait until then to discover what was inside. How could she get through the whole day at work wondering about its contents? So, gently she lifted the flap to expose a sheet of the same paper as the envelope. As she read the letter she gasped in amazement.

It was from a firm of solicitors in Hitchin, Hertfordshire, informing her that if she could visit them she would learn something to her advantage. Would she please telephone and make an appointment? It was signed by Andrew Underwood.

How strange, she did not know anyone from that area, though the name brought back some childish recollection of having visited someone way back in time - so long ago that the memory was almost extinct. She tried to recall the memory but the only thing that came to mind was a train journey and the station sign 'Hitchin'. She thought she must have been about five or six years old and thinking about it remembered some silly joke she had made to her mother about itching and scratching.

She turned to look at the clock and realised that she must hurry to get ready for work. She put her mug and plate in the sink and discarded her dressing gown to put on her drab shop uniform. Looking in the mirror, she thought how ugly it was in a dingy brown. She tried to brighten it up with a bright yellow ribbon in her hair.

The department store where she worked was a short bus-ride away from home. It was an old rambling building rather in need of some modernisation. It was situated on several levels and it was on the ground floor that she worked in the kitchen department.

The day passed slowly and when she was serving the customers her mind was only half on the task in hand. Once or twice the manager had had to correct her on something and this was very unusual. She was one of the best assistants he had.

During her tea-break she took the letter from her handbag and read it again - for the sixth time. She had read it three times when on the bus getting here and again when she had arrived. She was so excited. She would have liked to tell her friend, Susan, all about it but their tea-breaks had differed today and when on the shop floor they had no time to talk. As she had started later she would not be stopping for lunch but work through until five thirty.

At last it was time to go home and as she left the bus to walk along the dark street she hurried and broke into a little run. It had turned very cold now and she couldn't wait to be in the warm. When she entered the flat she kicked off her shoes and tossed her coat on the bed. She then made herself a cup of tea, and when she had finished it proceeded to wash and prepare the vegetables for the meal she and Joe shared in the evening. Having so little time to cook except at weekends she had bought a steak and kidney pie from the local butchers the previous day which she placed in the oven to heat. She was on tenterhooks and couldn't wait to show Joe the letter she had received. As soon as she heard his key in the lock she went to meet him.

It took only a few steps as the flat consisted of just a kitchen/diner and small living room all leading off from the small hallway. There was a bedroom that was politely described as a double by the letting agency but once the bed was in place it had only room for a tiny wardrobe and clothes were usually strewn around the place as it was not big enough to hold them all.

After kissing Joe gently on the lips Sally turned and picking up the letter handed it to him.

"Look what I got in the post, Joe. What do you think?"

"Can't it wait until I've eaten? I'm starving."

She was almost jumping up and down in her excitement.

"No, no it can't. Just read it. I'll dish up the dinner"

As Joe ran his eyes over the carefully written words he ran his fingers through his dark hair, which was a habit of his when something puzzled him. He then pursed his lips and let out a long slow whistle.

"Wow, that sounds exciting. I didn't know you had any rich relatives."

"Well, I haven't. That's the point. I know Mum is an only child and Dad had one brother. But he died without having any children. So there's no-one that I know of."

"Have you phoned your Mum and told her about the letter?"

"No, I wanted to wait until you got home to see what you think."

"Well, I should call her if I were you. She may know something."

Sally felt in her handbag for her purse and extracted some coins.

"I'll go down and use the phone now whilst it's quiet. Once all the others get in I'll never be able to get on it."

She slipped on the shoes that had been discarded earlier and put her coat round her shoulders. The hallway and stairway were not heated. She left the flat and ran down the stairs to the ground floor where the call box was situated and, after dialling, pressed the button to release the coins as her mother answered. The letter was in her hand and she explained as quickly as she possibly could before her money ran out. There was a silence at the other end of the line that seemed to penetrate the air and go on forever.

"Mum, Mum are you there?"

Her mother's voice seemed to come from faraway, which of course that's exactly what it was being over two hundred miles but Sally couldn't help feeling that something was wrong.

"Er, yes. I'm here. I can't really talk at the moment. Ring me when you've made the appointment with the solicitors and let me know how you get on."

Sally said "Goodbye" and put the phone back on it's cradle.

It would be too late in the day to telephone the solicitor now. She would call him tomorrow. As she made her way back up the stairs she couldn't help a feeling of unease. It wasn't like her mother not to find time to talk. She was usually only too pleased to chat. Sometimes she would tell Sally to reverse the charge so she didn't have to worry about running out of change.

The next morning just after nine o clock she telephoned Mr Underwood, the solicitor, at his office and speaking to his secretary made an appointment to meet up with him on the following Thursday. Joe arranged to have the day off work to accompany her.

***

The night before they were due to go to Hitchin Sally lay awake for what seemed like hours, the letter going over and over in her mind. What could it all be about? She was pleased when daylight at last appeared and she was able to get up and prepare a hasty breakfast for them both before setting off.

Sally was not the only one to have a sleepless night. Her mother, Mary, tossed and turned as thoughts and questions went racing through her mind. What would be the outcome of Sally's visit to the solicitors?. What would she discover? Would the secret that Mary had held close to her heart all these years be revealed? And if Sally found out the truth would she ever forgive her?

She loved her daughter so much and could not envisage having their relationship change from the loving one that it now was.

Trying to lie as still as possible so as not to disturb Jack her thoughts wandered back over the years. There was nothing she could do but wait. Wait for her beloved daughter to telephone her when she got home to find our what she had discovered.

They travelled on the underground to Kings Cross and Sally felt quite excited as they entered the station. It was bustling with men making their way to work most carrying the obligatory newspaper. This gave Sally an idea and whilst Joe queued to buy the tickets she made her way across to the book stall. She bought Joe a newspaper then ran her eyes over the magazines. She couldn't believe how many there were on every subject possible. She found it hard to choose just one. She never bought a magazine at home because she would not have had time to read one and this was a real luxury to her. There would be the odd one or two passed on to her by her friend but they were normally way out of date by the time she got them and when she thought of the ones she read in the dentist - well in mid-summer you'd be reading Christmas recipes and ideas for gifts. When she saw Joe walking across to her she quickly picked up a Woman's Own and paid the girl who was patiently waiting.

The thought of just sitting and reading on the train was something really special to her. She couldn't remember the last time she had had time to do it. Life was much too busy.

Beside her job in the department store she also did a little cleaning job two evenings a week in a local office so they could save a few pounds here and there towards a deposit on a house. Though at times she wondered whether they would ever have enough even if she did three jobs. It was a slow process and they always seemed to be dipping into their savings for something or other. It never had time to accumulate.

They had been together since they were at secondary school and they had married just after Sally's twenty first birthday. Now, a year later, they still felt they were on honeymoon and very much in love. For three months they had lived with Sally's parents and slept in Sally's old bedroom. They had all got on well together and would probably have stayed with them longer but Sally's father received an offer of a job in Yorkshire so it was left to Joe and Sally to find a flat. It was not exactly what they would have liked but it was wonderful to be in their own place.

Neither of them were familiar with this part of London and both felt quite a sense of adventure. They had half an hour to spare before the train was due and went across to the cafeteria and ordered two coffees. It was wonderful just to sit and watch the travellers coming and going.

Sally nearly gasped aloud when she saw some of the fashions. Some girls were dressed in the tiniest of mini skirts. Their legs must be freezing, Sally thought. She felt quite sedate in her own outfit. Before she knew it the half hour had sped by and they made their way to the right platform.

By this time the majority of people going to work had already left on their various trains and there were only a few travellers entering the one they were getting on. They managed to get a seat in a carriage on their own, but it wasn't long before it started to fill up. After two stops they had the company of an elderly couple, two teenagers, a stout blowsy woman wearing an old moth-eaten fur coat and a young mother with a toddler and baby. The poor mother was looking a bit harassed and was very appreciative when Sally offered to hold the baby whilst she put her bags on the rack above them.

Sally felt very proud to be sitting next to her handsome husband dressed in his best suit, which was, in fact, the only decent one he possessed. His unruly dark hair had been brushed back and held in place with a dash of Brylcreem. He did look nice, she thought. Joe was also thinking along the same lines. Sally was wearing her red winter coat and her dark hair with its auburn tints was tied back in a pony tail with a matching red ribbon. In his eyes she looked quite beautiful.

She opened her magazine and tried to concentrate on an article about kitchen design but found she was intrigued with all the houses flying by. There were factories with tall chimneys quite unpleasing to the eye but in no time at all they were in the countryside.

Sally felt quite sorry for the young mother as the toddler began to get tired of sitting still. He had flung his book on the floor.

"Would you like me to read to him?" she offered.

"Oh, yes please. If you wouldn't mind. He does get bored. We're going to visit my mother."

So he snuggled up beside her Sally, his thumb in his mouth as he listened intently. It wasn't long before she realised he was fast asleep. She lowered the book to the seat and cuddled him. The young mother smiled at her.

The child slept for twenty minutes and woke completely refreshed and wanting another story. Their stop was the one before Sally's and she felt a reluctance to let the little boy go. She couldn't wait to have one of her own but knew, in their present circumstances it would be a long time before they had the room. The elderly couple smiled at her as she helped the young mother get her things together and handed the child over.

As she took her seat again beside Joe he took her hand in his and squeezed it. She smiled up at him and felt so happy she could burst. The elderly lady opposite smiled as she looked at them. They made such a handsome couple and were obviously so much in love. She and her husband beside her had always had a happy marriage and she couldn't help but feel a pang of envy for this young couple just starting out on life. "Time goes far too quickly," she thought. "I hope they make the most of every minute."

2

As the train slowed down and the station came into view they saw the sign 'Hitchin' and eagerly jumped up from their seats. When finally they came to a stop Joe leaned out of the window to release the latch on the door. Then he held her hand as she jumped down onto the platform. They handed over their tickets and as they left the station Sally looked at the hastily drawn map that the solicitor had sent them. They were to walk along Walsworth Road to the end, cross over Hermitage Road and then turn right just before the Market Square into Portmill Lane.

The air was chill and Sally was glad of her warm coat. She thought of those young girls in their mini-skirts. It was the first day of November and the leaves were in full autumn colour. As they came out of the station they saw a row of cottages up a slope to their right and a flour mill across the road. Further along was a car showroom and a furniture shop before one or two small shops. Once they had passed a row of terraced houses on their left they came to a greengrocers and like a couple of excited school children they went inside and bought two rosy apples which they crunched as they walked. They noticed that the houses became larger, some quite grand. Sally thought it quite beautiful when they reached a wooded area with large Victorian houses on the other side. The air was filled with the smell of fires burning as the aroma rose from the numerous chimneys and hung on the misty air. On their right they saw a wooded area opening up to a steep grass covered hill. It was called Windmill Hill they were to learn later, though there was no sign of a windmill. If there had ever been it was now long gone.

The solicitors office was situated in Portmill Lane and as they turned into the road they could see, not far away, St Mary's Church. It was a magnificent building with grass leading down to the river. A beautiful weeping willow stood over-hanging the water.

Joe and Sally looked at the numbers and located the door leading to Andrew Underwood's office. They stepped into the warmth of the building and were immediately assailed with the wonderful smell of beeswax polish. The hallway was panelled in dark oak which shone with years of loving care. They were directed up the wooden staircase by a grey-haired upright lady and came upon a door which opened onto a large office. When a voice bade them enter they tentatively opened the door and it was as though they were stepping back into the past. The room looked as though it had been trapped in a time warp. A rich red carpet covered the floor and dark oak panelling lined the walls. Hanging on them were portraits of past dignitaries. The largest and grandest one which hung in the centre of the wall above the fireplace, Sally was to discover at a later date, was of Andrew Underwood's grandfather who had started the business back in the last century.

The centre of the room was dominated by a large ornate walnut desk, the green leather top of which was almost covered with sheets of paper. Sally's eye was caught by a beautiful pen holder carved in ivory. When turning to the window, draped in red velvet curtains, she caught a glimpse of the church standing proud amongst the trees. They had never been in a room so grand.

Mr Underwood, the solicitor, with his white hair and large bushy moustache looked as though he had been there since the place was built.

He indicated for them to sit and asked if they would like coffee. They both felt out of their depth and were unsure how to answer. Joe managed to find his voice and spoke up saying they would love one.

When Sally tried to remember the next half hour later in the day, her mind was a haze. She had been so surprised by the news that she was in shock. Mr Underwood informed her that she had been left the legacy of a house in the very road they had walked along fifteen minutes earlier. She just couldn't believe it.

When she asked him who had left it to her she was told it was Mrs Ellen Bancroft.

"But, I've never heard of her." Sally protested, in surprise. "There must be a mistake."

The old man reached across his desk and placed a gnarled hand on hers. He had taken an instant liking to this girl. There was a freshness about her that he found appealing.

"I can assure you, my dear, there is no mistake. She certainly must have heard of you. Now as soon as you have proved beyond doubt that you are indeed Sally Jane Westwood nee Bolton, then you will have the keys to the property. It will take a couple of weeks to complete all the formalities, but in the meantime I can take you along to see the property if you wish."

If she wished! Sally could hardly contain herself. She turned to Joe and his hand took hers.

She found it difficult to answer; her mouth had gone dry. She at last managed to get the words out.

"I would love to see it, please Mr Underwood."

"Then so you shall, me dear."

As he got up from his seat and went through to his secretary there was a lightness in his step that had not been there before. He had set out from home this morning with a heavy heart. He had recently lost his dear wife after a long illness but this young girl had put new spirit into him. He was so used to dealing with truculent clients, who never showed any appreciation for what he did, that it was such a pleasant change to have someone who showed such happiness and pleasure in her good fortune that it had renewed his faith in human nature.

Although they could easily have walked to the house in under ten minutes he took Joe and Sally in his car, which looked as old as he, Sally thought. It was an old Austin Seven and Joe couldn't hide his delight as they climbed into it. The seats were of green leather and the whole inside smelled of age - a smell that is unique to old cars. Joe breathed deeply as he took in the aroma. After only a few minutes, which Joe wished could have been hours they pulled onto the drive of a large Victorian semi-detached house.

Sally looked up at the imposing red brick building and thought it wonderful. There was ivy growing in abundance up the front of it and the large sash windows looked dark. Joe had laughed when Sally said later that she thought it looked rather sad.

They walked past a large forsythia bush which still showed the odd yellow flower defying the cold, up three stone steps to a porch and turning to their left were facing a large door. The green paint on it was peeling and looked very neglected. When they entered, it felt cold and damp. Andrew Underwood saw her shiver and spoke softly.

"It's been standing empty for a few months. It needs warming up a bit. I'm afraid the heating system is a bit antiquated. I've known the house for many years and I can assure you that once you have got it round it will be a wonderful home. Oh, I forgot to tell you that Mrs. Bancroft also left you some funds to spend on it."

They had walked into a hallway with Victorian tiles on the floor and saw to their right a sweeping staircase covered in a red patterned carpet leading up from it. Opposite them was a door with another to their left. Leading down from the hallway was another staircase, less imposing than the other and bare of carpet. As they went through the door on the left they saw a long room with a large white fireplace at the end. There were two windows that had the old fashioned shutters on them. These were closed, making the room very dark. Andrew Underwood immediately strode across to them and lowering the shutters let the late morning sunshine stream in. The whole room was transformed. It was quite beautiful. In the centre stood a large oval table which, though covered in a light layer of dust, still showed the grandeur of a bygone era. Sally was quite breathless. It was all she'd ever dreamed of. And it was hers. She couldn't believe it.

The second room was similar, though more square, and the fireplace was of black marble. There was only one large sash window and Sally couldn't resist a peep out of it. What she saw took her breath away. It was a beautiful old walled garden which was very neglected and overgrown. The grass was a least a foot high and stinging nettles were everywhere but it still held a kind of magic for her. The trees held a touch of frost on their branches, which added to the beauty.

As they travelled on up the stairs going from one room to another Sally was speechless. They passed an office in which stood a large desk with numerous drawers, each with a small brass handle. They looked so inviting that Sally longed to open them and look inside. Leather bound books lined two walls and from the sash window Sally could see the garden.

They continued up the stairs where, on the first floor there were three bedrooms. The one at the back of the house was obviously the one where the old lady had slept. It still held all her personal belongings. Sally felt as though she was intruding on someone else's privacy; as though she had stepped into a room that was still occupied.

On the dressing table lay a beautiful silver-backed hair brush and matching mirror with perfume bottles of every colour and design surrounded it. The bed was made up and covered with a heavy satin eiderdown in deep pink. There was even a silk robe still draped over the back of a chair as though it had just been placed there a few moments earlier. Ellen Bancroft's presence was almost tangible and Sally gave a little shiver, not because it was cold but because she felt there was someone standing next to her, almost touching.

Although the rest of the house seemed cold and unloved, this room was different. It had a warm feel to it. Sally had the strangest feeling that she had come home.

After a quick look in the other two bedrooms on this floor they made their way up to the top of the house. Here were two more large rooms quite sparsely furnished, the back room looking out onto the garden and the front one facing the road. When Sally opened another door she found a long narrow room full of old furniture and trunks. It was quite dark and she didn't go in far. She shivered again but this time she did feel cold; it was eerily cold. She quickly closed the door again.

She went back into one of the bedrooms and looked out again onto the garden. She was very high up and from here got a wonderful view of it. Where the grass had not obscured the view she could see tiny paths lined with miniature box hedges. From up here the trees looked even more beautiful. To her right she caught sight of a magnificent old building just visible amongst the trees which, she was later to discover, was The Convent, a Catholic school for young ladies.

When, at last, she managed to tear herself away from the window, they went downstairs and continued down the winding stairs that lead to the semi-basement. Here there was a kitchen and scullery with a door leading out onto the garden. There was even a large coal cellar with a chute to let the coal down from outside. Sally only had a quick look down there. It was very dark as the only light came from a tiny window which was very grimy. She thought it a bit creepy. She would let Joe get the coal when it was needed.

She would have loved to go out into the garden but felt, as it was still very cold, it was not fair on this kindly old gentlemen to make him go outside so she decided it would have to wait until another time. She still could not believe that this was going to be her and Joe' s home. It had not quite sunk in yet.

They spent nearly an hour looking round and taking it all in and by the time they walked back down the front steps to the car, Sally felt she had known the house forever, so at home did she feel. She couldn't wait for the next two weeks to pass.

They went back to Andrew's office where they were offered another welcome coffee to warm themselves up. They then said their goodbyes and walked back to the station to catch their train. Luckily, it was a buffet train so they were able to have a snack on board. They sat in silence, which was unusual for them, but both were lost in thought. They still could not believe their good fortune.

As she and Joe entered their flat they couldn't help but feel how small it was. It would have fitted into the basement of the house at Walsworth Road. When at last they got into bed that night Joe took her into his arms and they made love, not with the passion that they usually felt but in a slow loving way and when Sally finally turned away from him and tucked herself down she breathed in contentment. It had been such a magical day and she knew that this was just the start.

Sally was not the only one who was feeling content at that moment for as Andrew Underwood sat up in his bed propped up on the pillows and sipping his creamy cup of cocoa there was a feeling of well-being that he had not experienced for weeks.

After Joe and Sally had left his office he called in his secretary and set to preparing the paperwork that would secure them the property in Walsworth Road and when that was done to his satisfaction he got into his car and set of home to his house in Gray's Lane.

It had been a lonely house since his wife had died and this was the first time since then that he had not dreaded entering it without her welcome. He couldn't explain it even to himself but there was a new lease of life in him.

He had been very fond of Ellen Bancroft and, after losing his wife, her death had been a double blow. He had also felt her presence as he had shown Joe and Sally round the house and knew without a shadow of a doubt that she would have been very pleased with today's happenings.

Sally really was a breath of fresh air in his musty old world and he couldn't wait to see her again. She had obviously loved the house and Andrew knew she would be happy there. It was a house very close to his heart. For many years he had crossed the threshhold. William and Ellen had been far more than clients - they had been good friends.

He had met William and Ellen when as a young man he had just entered his father's business. Returning from his final year at law school he was buoyed up with youthful enthusiasm. They had been the first clients his father allowed him to attend and they had stayed with him ever since. There was not much about their lives that he did not know. And now he must keep counsel for there were things that could not be told. Not yet.

3

August 1896

As Ellen gradually came to consciousness she stretched and opened her eyes to a bright morning. She lifted her head to look at the small brass clock on the mantle-shelf. It was just after eight o'clock and she could see the sun had risen and although her room, being at the back of the house, did not get much sun until the afternoon, she could see through her delicate curtains that it was bright outside.

The room was papered in pale lemon so, even if the day was dull, she always got the impression of sunshine. But today it was really shining. There was one sash window in the bedroom, which was situated on the second floor of the house overlooking the garden. She loved the view from this window and would often stand and gaze out on, what she considered, the best place in the world. She had grown up in this house and had never known any other.

When they had moved into it she had been only a year old and had grown with the garden. Her father had planted numerous trees that were now grown into magnificent species. The fruit trees, at this time of year, were laden with apples, pears, plums and damsons. The large cherry tree had long been picked of it's harvest but still stood proud. From the window she could see Mr Barnard's orchard that lay over the wall at the end of the garden. The trees were dotted with tiny red apples. These were especially delicious and although they had four apple trees of their own she and her brother, Samuel, had, as children, often climbed over the wall to take a few of these forbidden fruits to eat. They were succulently sweet.

At the end of the garden was a tall fir tree where a swing hung from a branch that jutted out. Ellen had spent many an hour on that swing going so high she could see over the tall red brick wall into next door's garden.

If she craned her neck and looked to the right she could see The Convent, a magnificent old building surrounded by trees. Often when walking by this school she wished she could have attended there as the girls would parade in their white dresses on special saints days. She envied them so much. They all looked so pretty.

As she became fully awake Ellen realised why she was feeling such excitement. It was her sixteenth birthday and she was to have a party. She threw back the covers and leapt out of bed, and in doing so dislodged the hot water bottle which clattered to the floor. It was made of heavy pottery and would be a comfort on chill nights, but the water had long cooled and as she bent to pick it up she shuddered at its coldness.

Picking up her robe from the chair where she had draped it the night before she slipped her arms into it and tied the ribbons at the neck. The robe was a fancy one with ruffles and pink bows down the front. Being nearly the end of August the air was still warm enough to wear something so frivolous. She would make the most of it because in the next few weeks it would grow much colder and large houses were not the most comfortable places to live in. As the days grew shorter she would have to wear sensible, warm garments. Flannelette would be the material that underwear and nightclothes would be made from.

Before she left her room she picked up her hairbrush and ran it quickly through her long auburn hair which fell in waves around her shoulders. Her mother was very particular how Ellen looked, even first thing in the morning.

She ran down the stairs, along the landing, and on reaching the next flight lifted her left leg over and slid down the curving balustrade. This she had done since she had been old enough to balance, much to her mother's consternation. Perhaps, she thought, now she had reached the mature age of sixteen she would cease. But on the other hand, perhaps not. It was, after all, one of her favourite activities.

As she went down the lower flight of stairs she lifted her nose to the air. She could smell bacon frying and realised just how hungry she felt. On entering the kitchen she kissed her mother lightly on the cheek. Her mother turned. "My, you are up early today. I wonder why."

"Oh, Mother. I'm so excited. I can't wait for my party to start."

"I keep telling you, darling, do not wish your time away. This is probably one of the best days of your life. Make the most of every minute."

Her mother placed a plate in front of her on which lay two rashers of bacon and a fried egg. Toast lay on a plate to her left and cup of tea on her right. She thought she was far too excited to eat but after the first mouthful enjoyed every last crumb. As she finished it and made to go back upstairs her mother detained her with trivial talk. Ellen was actually itching to go back up to her bedroom to dress but knew it would be rude to leave her mother in mid-sentence.

When eventually she reached her bedroom and opened the door she realised why her mother had kept her talking. Across the room was a large parcel wrapped awkwardly in brown paper. She quickly tore the paper away and gasped when she saw a beautiful cheval mirror.

It was made of carved wood and painted pure white. There were little touches of gold paint added. It was breathtaking. And even more so when she spied her reflection in it. She saw this lovely girl with long dark hair tumbling over her shoulders. Her eyes were sparkling and her cheeks were suffused with pink from her running up the stairs matching the ribbons adorning her robe. She then realised her mother and father were behind her watching her reaction.

"Oh, thank you, thank you. It is so beautiful."

Her father came forward to kiss her. "Happy Birthday, darling. May you gaze in this mirror for many years and see the lovely person you see now."

From that moment the mirror took pride of place in her bedroom and never a day passed that she didn't look into it. It reflected her every changing mood.

Through the years to come it watched her. It shared her joys and sorrows. It saw her laughter and tears. It saw all.

4

December 1963

The move into their house was, for Joe and Sally, the most exciting time they had ever shared. They supervised the loading of the large van that was to take their belongings, then hurriedly made their way to the underground station. When reaching Kings Cross they were relieved to board their train and sink into their seats. The journey was harder this time as they had luggage to contend with and were more than relieved when at last they turned into the gateway of the house and walked up the drive. It was a bitterly cold day and as they entered the front door Sally shivered.

"It's even colder than before. Look, you can see our breath. Let's light the fire before we do anything else. I'm keeping my coat on until it's warmed up a bit."

It wasn't long before Joe had fires lit in most of the rooms. He had made numerous trips down to the coal cellar and brought up scuttles full of coal. The cellar was reached through a door leading off the old hallway in the basement. There was no artificial light down there and the only glimpse of light came through the small window. The ability to fill the scuttles was more luck than judgement and many a time Joe swore as he twisted his ankle on lumps of coal. He must, he resolved, buy a good torch.

Now, as they sat in front of a blazing fire in the lounge drinking a welcome cup of tea he felt it had been well worth the effort. Even so it was some time before they removed their warm coats for it seemed to take forever for the warmth to penetrate the air.

The removal men arrived in the afternoon and set to unloading their few pieces of furniture. The modern sofa and chairs looked quite out of place in the large lounge and Sally vowed to get rid of them as soon as possible. If they had not had to clear the flat out they would have left them behind and now she wished she had got the second-hand shop to collect them.

The bedroom they had chosen was the large one on the first floor, the one that Ellen had occupied. There was already a large oak wardrobe in there and a matching chest of drawers. Andrew Underwood had arranged for the room to be cleaned and the bed made up. He had not cleared it completely of Ellen's personal belongings as he felt she would have wanted it to look homely and welcoming for Sally. So he had left the silver-backed hair brush set and her perfume bottles on the dressing table. With the fire blazing in the grate it looked very inviting and as Sally drew the rich velvet curtains across she looked out over the garden. It was white with a severe frost and breathtakingly beautiful.

By the time the removal van had left, darkness had already descended upon them. The kitchen cupboards were bare except for essentials so Joe suggested he find a fish and chip shop. Whilst he was gone Sally made a pot of tea which she set on a tray and carried into the dining room. They had not unpacked any of their crockery but there had been no need as the cupboards were filled with everything they could need.

On the dresser against the wall was a whole set of dinner plates, tea plates and saucers with cups hanging on the hooks. She chose the dainty cups which were adorned with pink roses. She wasn't sure about Joe's reaction but they were so beautiful and like nothing she had used before. He did make some derogatory remark when he returned with the delicious smelling fish and chips about only having two mouthfuls but, as Sally told him, there was plenty more in the pot.

They sat and ate their fill by the roaring fire. There were little leather covered seats on each end of the fender so they roasted one side of their bodies, then, giggling like a couple of school children, changed places to warm the other. They had to tear themselves away from it to climb the stairs to their bedroom. Feeling exhausted from their long day they tumbled into bed.

The fire Joe had lit in the bedroom was still burning and they huddled close to keep warm, watching the reflection of the flames on the ceiling. Neither had ever slept in a bedroom with a fire before and it was an experience they would treasure for many years.

Sally was still puzzled as to why she had been singled out to inherit the house and felt sure her mother knew something she was not telling. She had tried to speak to her on the phone a couple of times but had got no nearer to knowing the truth.

Oh well, she would just enjoy it whilst she could as she still had the uneasy feeling that it was all a mistake and it would be taken away from her.

***

As Sally and Joe were warm and snug in their bed, Donald Bancroft sat in the small, dingy room that he was renting. He was seething with anger. He had planned everything down to the smallest detail and here he was with nothing. The old lady had only left him a paltry sum to tide him over.

He had been so sure that he would inherit the house. His parents were in Canada and they had never shown any inclination to live back here. His Aunt Susannah was also out there with his cousin, Patricia, and she had no children. So where the hell had this girl come from? He could not believe it when he had been escorted from the house where he had been living for the past two years. He had been treated like a criminal. Apparently there had been a letter left by his grandmother at her solicitors saying that if anything happened to her he should leave the house immediately.

So here he was in this godforsaken place. The room was devoid of any comforts. There was just a bed and a small wardrobe. The kitchen he had to share with three other occupants but he did little cooking. Most of the meagre wages he got in his mundane job was spent on gambling and the odd bottle of whisky. Food was way down on his list of priorities.

He had planned everything down to the last detail and now this slip of a girl had appeared out of the blue and got everything that should have been his. Well, he wasn't going to sit back and let her get away with it. He would bide his time and do whatever was necessary to get his rewards. He had given the last five years to his grandmother waiting for her to die and in the end he had had to give her a helping hand. Well, he wasn't going to give up now.

5

December 1897

It was a cold, crisp December evening. Every light in the house had been lit and every room was aglow. The lights ranged from gas lamps, oil lamps and candles, each one giving it's own distinctive smell and radiance to the room in which it was situated. The colours that radiated from the ladies attire was akin to a rainbow swirling around as the guests mingled. Dresses of every hue in fabrics that shone - especially the silks and satins.

Ellen was dressed in green velvet, which hung in folds with a small bustle at the back. Green had always been her favourite colour as it enhanced the auburn tints in her hair.

Crinolines had gone out of fashion and perhaps it was just as well, Ellen thought, for the guests would not have had room to move in wide skirts. Although the rooms were of good proportion, with so many people squeezing into the house for the party it was full to the brim.

Huge fires burned in the two main rooms and doors were left open to bring some warmth to the rest of the house.

Ellen was running up and down stairs to help her mother bring refreshments to the dining room, which wasn't easy in her heavy velvet skirt. She had to try and hold it up with one hand whilst she carried laden plates There was not the space to have a sit-down meal but the table was covered with platters holding tiny delicacies of mouth watering flavours. Three young girls had been at the house all day in preparation of these but May, Ellen's mother, had said they could go home and enjoy the New Year celebrations with their own families. They would be back in the morning to help with the clearing up.

As Ellen was struggling to carry a large bowl of punch into the room a deep voice came to her ears.

"Can I help? That looks rather large for you to manage."

Ellen turned and gratefully relinquished the bowl into the hands of an extremely handsome young man with the darkest eyes she had ever seen. He was dressed all in black but it did not make him look sombre in any way. The black velvet evening jacket only made him look even more handsome with his dark hair and deep brown eyes. She caught her breath and managed to answer him in a calm voice.

"Why, thank you. I think I was just about to drop it and that would have been a disaster. It is Father's favourite punch."

The bowl was placed in the centre of the large table and tiny glasses were hung around it. From it came the wonderful aroma of fruits and alcohol and on top floated tiny pieces of sugared pineapple.

"Would you like a glass for your trouble, Sir?"

"Please do not call me Sir. It makes me feel ancient and I am barely older than you. Thank you. It smells delicious. Let me introduce myself. I'm William, but my friends call me Will so I hope you will do so. I work with your father."

"Oh, I'm Ellen - but of course you must know that if you know my Father." She felt foolish but thankfully he didn't seem to notice.

He said "Yes. He often speaks of you. He is very proud of his daughter."

"I really don't know why. I haven't done much to merit any praise. I suppose I am just a dutiful daughter who abides by his rules and shares his ideas. He is a very kind father and even though he is always busy at the printing works he finds time to talk to me. We have many discussions in the evenings. He is quite modern in his thinking. Oh, I'm sorry. I must get back to helping mother."

William reluctantly let her go with the parting words "Perhaps we can talk again later."

She smiled at him. "I'd like that."

Returning to the kitchen she had a lightness in her step and her mother couldn't help but notice the flush in her cheeks.

As they sat side by side, eating and talking, Ellen forgot any shyness she had first felt as the evening progressed with everyone enjoying themselves and they had, by the time the New Year had been rung in, forged a friendship that was to last many years.

Her mother had persuaded her to play the pianoforte but, unusually for her, she felt rather nervous and chose simple pieces to entertain their guests. It pleased her that Will sang along standing beside her. He had a fine baritone voice and received quite an applause when he finished a rendering of The Ash Grove.

When the guests had departed and Ellen finally climbed into bed she was aglow. Perhaps it was the wine she had been allowed to drink, she thought.

Or more likely the memory of the person who had dominated her evening. She thought Will the most handsome man she had ever met. All through the night he penetrated her dreams and on awaking she really felt as though the new year was starting out on a wonderful note and could only get better.

During the next few months Will became a regular visitor to the house and many a happy day, when he wasn't working, was spent in his company. They would walk through the recreation parks, her arm in his and on fine Sundays he would borrow her father's car and take her to Bedford where they would row on the river.

On the anniversary of their meeting on New Years Eve he presented her with a gold ring set with an emerald and asked her to marry him. He had already spoken to her parents and got their consent. They were delighted.

They were married at St. Mary's Church in September and travelled to Venice for their honeymoon on The Orient Express. When they returned a month later it was decided, as Will had to travel abroad a lot with his father, and this would have meant Ellen spending a lot of time alone, that they would live with her parents at the house in Walsworth Road.

They were given the back bedroom on the first floor. Like her previous bedroom it also overlooked the garden so Ellen was more than happy. She loved Will dearly and was over the moon when her their first child was born in January 1900. It was on a cold winter day but with a fire burning in the hearth Ellen felt she was in heaven. It was a boy and they named him Daniel.

The cheval mirror reflected the birth.

6

January 1964

The snow lay over the garden giving a magical feel. It was two or three inches thick on the branches of the trees. As Sally drew back the curtains she gasped. She still couldn't believe this was all hers. They had been here for just over a month now but to Sally it felt like she had been here years. The house had completely captivated her.

Although it had been closed up for only a few months the cold seemed to have penetrated the whole place and no matter how many fires they lit, when they moved away from them, the air was still cold.

Sally pulled open a drawer and took out two thick jumpers and pulled them both on. She wore tights under her trousers and thick socks. She smiled then as she thought how she had changed since moving in. Before, when alone with Joe she would always try to wear sexy clothes. Now, even in bed, she had to wear warm pyjamas. She made her way down to the kitchen. The range had been banked up before they had gone to bed and the room felt warm. She did a lot of the cooking in here if she could, although there was an antiquated gas stove in the scullery which she could use, if need be. The breakfast was ready on the table by the time Joe came into the room.

"We'll have to get this heating sorted out. I've never been so cold." he grumbled.

"I know, darling. I'll ask around and see who we can find to sort it out. Perhaps Mr Underwood can recommend someone. I want to go through the box-room and bring some more furniture down but I can't face it up there in this cold. I did find a little fan heater in the cupboard though, so if there is a socket up there we could plug that in. I want you to come up with me though. That room gives me the creeps."

"Right, we'll start it today. Tomorrow I've got an interview to get through. The money is getting a bit tight. It won't last forever."

The box room seemed even colder than the rest of the house but as they rummaged amongst the odd assortment of furniture and boxes they found the cold and discomfort was forgotten. It was like Aladdin's cave. Most of the furniture was old and out of date and some beyond repair. Joe suggested they chop most of it up for firewood to keep them warm but there was the odd thing or two they came across that looked interesting. Joe found tools and suchlike which he was very interested in and Sally left him to sort these out. She was far more intrigued when she came across various toys that had long been forgotten in time. She saw visions of the children who must have played with them long ago. There was a beautiful doll's house and beside it a box of tiny furniture all carefully wrapped. She couldn't wait to get it down stairs and play with it. It was the one thing she had loved to play with when small but the little one her mother had bought her when she was about seven years old was nothing compared to this one.

Apart from short breaks for coffee and a hasty lunch they had been in the box room for over six hours and darkness had again fallen before they made their way downstairs. Sally ran a bath and she quickly washed down and leapt out again. It was too cold to linger in the bathroom. Joe followed suit and when they were both ensconced in their dressing gowns they sat up in their bed each holding a mug of cocoa and watching the flames of the fire flickering on the ceiling.

Sally had come across an old-fashioned hot water bottle made of heavy porcelain and had filled it. When she showed it to Joe he burst out laughing. He had seen these things in museums but had never actually held one. It felt heavy and cumbersome.

"If you're going to laugh I shall keep it to myself and you can be cold."

"No, no. I take it back. Come on let's go and try it out.

And so the strange object lay down at their feet between them giving a bit of warmth to the cold sheets.

Tomorrow, Sally vowed she would go down to the town and buy an electric blanket. Why hadn't she thought of that before? The trouble is, she thought, they would never want to get out of bed.

7

1907

Ellen crept into her daughter's room and stood looking at her for about three minutes. Today was her birthday. She was five years old.

Thinking back to the day she was born gave Ellen such a feeling of joy. Daniel had always been such a discontented baby. He had always craved attention and since his sister came on the scene it had got worse. The jealousy he felt reared its ugly head continually and Ellen was hard-pressed not to retaliate. She tried to understand. After all, his little world had been invaded by this tiny being who held everyone captivated. She only had to smile and people fell in love with her. Ellen often thought that if Daniel smiled more he would be so much more popular.

Susannah was even smiling in her sleep. She was obviously dreaming of something pleasant. As she turned her head on the pillow and her hair came over her face, Ellen gently pushed it back and the child opened her eyes. As soon as she came to consciousness she sat up and hugged her mother tight.

"Mummy, it's my birthday."

"I know, my darling. Isn't it exciting?"

"Yes, and I am going to have a party."

Susannah was wearing her new party dress of green satin. It had a full skirt and tiny velvet bows adorning the front of the bodice. She twirled in front of her mother's cheval mirror, standing on tip toe to capture the full effect. Her hair hung in ringlets tied with a matching green ribbon. Oh, how she had suffered earlier today when Mummy had put rags in her hair to create the ringlets, but she decided now that it had been worth it. She felt like a princess.

She climbed onto the stool near the kidney shaped dressing table to look in her mother's jewellery box. She loved going through her mother's trinkets. One or two pieces were quite valuable but Susanna was too young to be aware of that. She just loved running her fingers through the colours and placing the earrings in pairs. Sometimes she would create a face made up of the pieces on the white bed coverlet.

Today, though, she had too much else on her mind to bother with faces. It was her fifth birthday and she was to have a party. Balloons had been blown up and hung around the dining room and the table had been set with pretty plates and dishes to hold the tiny cakes and jellies that she had helped Nelly, the cook, to make. She loved helping Nelly in the kitchen. Nelly was very patient with her and didn't grumble when she made a mess, which she often did.

She had eight friends coming to her party and her daddy had arranged for a real magician to come along and perform for them. He would do lots of tricks and pull coloured handkerchiefs from his pockets. Susannah had seen one before when she had gone with her mother and brother to the theatre on a day trip to London. That had been really exciting and to have her own magician for her party made her feel very special.

She heard her mother calling her so ran down the stairs to where she and her father were waiting in the lounge. Her brother Daniel was also standing near them. He was scowling as usual. He often did when Susannah was getting the attention but she was too excited to care. They all looked at her and she wasn't quite sure what she was meant to do. And then she saw the large parcel standing by the table.

"Happy Birthday, darling." her mother and father chorused. "Go on. Open it."

She tore off the paper to reveal the most perfect doll's house which was the exact replica of the one they were in, even down to the matching curtains. It was so beautiful that she felt like crying. She opened the front of the house and peeped inside. There was her bedroom with her tiny bed and when she looked through the back windows she could see the room they were in now. And to top it all there were little people just like them. She fingered each in turn then turned to her mother to hug her.

"Thank you, Mummy and Daddy. Thank you!".

For a while her party was forgotten as she took out the furniture in the doll's house and then replaced it again. This she did several times before Daniel got tired of her enjoying herself and kicked the pieces, scattering them over the carpet.

By the time the small guests had arrived he was in a filthy mood. He hated it when Susannah got all the attention.

When they had eaten as much as they could they were sent into the garden to play and when they were called back in it was to see that a little stage had been set up and there in his long robe of red and gold was Miko, the magician. He wore a matching pointed hat and held a silver wand in his hand .

The children sat enthralled for an hour, never moving unless he asked one of them to assist him. It was always one of the girls he asked and again Daniel was furious. Why wasn't he chosen? He was far more important being the only boy there.

By the time Miko had finished his act the floor was strewn with coloured squares and ribbons. It was magical.

Daniel was in an even worse mood than before. He swore he would get his own back for being neglected.

8

1964

It was in early March when Sally first began to hear the strange sounds. Joe was at work and she was alone in the house. She had just stripped the bed for washing when something made her stop and listen. She hadn't left the radio on so it couldn't be that. The sounds seemed to come from upstairs. She left the bedroom and crept along the landing. It sounded like footsteps. She went cold. There was someone upstairs. She dared not go up but retreated back along the landing and scooping up the washing hurried down the stairs to the scullery.

They had had the telephone re-connected but who could she ring? Her mother perhaps. Yes, that's what she would do. She wouldn't tell her she was scared - just make an excuse to phone. Of course, she could invite her to stay. It had been mentioned but nothing had come of it. Well now she would make sure it was arranged.

It was good to talk to someone and took her mind off the sounds and by the end of the conversation her mother had, reluctantly it seemed to Sally, agreed to visit in five days time. There were no further sounds so Sally put it down to her vivid imagination.

It was two days later when she had a caller. On opening the door she saw a man on the doorstep. She guessed he was around forty years old with mousey brown hair just starting to turn grey. She was aware of his piercing blue eyes that seemed to penetrate her. He was grossly overweight and his clothes were crumpled. She felt a feeling of unease and took an instant dislike to him. Then she told herself not to be so stupid and forced a smile.

"Good morning. Can I help you?"

He shifted uncomfortably from one foot to the other. "Yes, I've come to see the lady of the house."

Sally felt quite grand being addressed so. She gave an little embarrassed laugh.

"Well, that's me. What can I do for you?"

She felt she should ask him in but for some uneasy reason was reluctant to do so. So she waited for him to answer.

"Well, it's a bit awkward to introduce myself. I'm not sure just how I am related to you. I'm Donald Bancroft. Ellen Bancroft was my grandmother and I lived here and looked after her until she died."

He said this rather in a truculent tone like a little boy who had been refused a treat.

"Oh, I see. Sorry, I didn't realise who you were. Won't you come in?"

She reluctantly opened the door wide enough for him to enter, still feeling uneasy but not knowing quite what else she could do. Should she offer him a cup of tea? Deciding it would be the only polite thing to do she showed him into the lounge before going downstairs to make it. She put some biscuits on a plate and carried the tray back up, placing it on the coffee table.

As they drank, conversation was stilted. She knew he was probing but could tell him nothing as that was precisely what she knew - nothing. She told him she had no idea why Ellen Bancroft should have left her the house. She had never heard of Ellen Bancroft until she had visited the solicitor.

She thought that she should feel sorry for him as it was obvious that he had expected the house to become his, but she still felt the dislike for him that she had first experienced.

She noticed that besides his clothes being creased and shabby, his shoes badly in need of a bit of polish and there was a damp smell that seemed to exude from him. She couldn't wait for him to go.

As she told Joe later, she had been relieved when the man had left. There had been an atmosphere whilst he had been here. She knew it was silly but she had felt scared. She wouldn't ask him in again if he called unless Joe was here.

The next day she decided to make an appointment with Mr Underwood to see if he could shed any light on Donald Bancroft.

Andrew Underwood gave her such a warm welcome that she felt quite overcome. He ushered into his office and ordered coffee.

"How are you, my dear? I've been meaning to call on you but didn't like to intrude. You must have been busy. Have you both settled In?"

"Yes, thank you. Joe has got a job at the local flour mill and is loving it. Not far to go either so he can walk there. We have settled in fine. Though mind you" she added with a grimace "we're glad the weather has warmed up. It was so cold there in the winter."

His receptionist entered with the coffee and he poured two cups.

"Well, what is the reason for your visit. Is there something I can do for you?"

"Yes, Mr Underwood. I had a caller, Donald Bancroft, and I wonder if you could tell me anything about him. It was a bit awkward, you see. He made me feel like an intruder. Questioned me on how I knew Ellen Bancroft. Well, as you know, I didn't. Can you tell me anything about him and have you *any* idea why she left me the house?"

Andrew looked a little uncomfortable and ran his finger round his stiffly starched collar as though it had suddenly become extra tight. He cleared his throat to delay in answering.

"Hm, hm. There are confidences I cannot disclose, but I will say do not encourage him. Ellen did not trust him and that is why he had to leave the house when she died."

"Leave the house? But why?"

"I am not sure, but there must have been some reason why she didn't trust him. I held a letter from Ellen to give the instruction that should anything happen to her he was to leave the house. If you want to, we could get a court order issued to keep him away."

Sally was appalled. "Oh, I'm sure that won't be necessary. But thank you all the same."

"Well, my dear." Andrew Underwood said as she left. "Just keep in touch and let me know if I can do anything for you."

"I will, and thank you again."

They had spent a pleasant half an hour whilst he told her some of the history of the town. He was very knowledgeable and obviously had a very keen interest in it all. He then showed her some old photographs, one of which was Hermitage Road at the turn of the century. What was now a busy shopping area had then been a beautiful avenue of trees. This, she thought a few minutes later, as she crossed the road, was what it must have been like in Ellen Bancroft's time. She stood for a few seconds as she crossed trying to envisage it but try as hard as she might she did not have much success. It was all so changed.

The old gentleman stood at the window and watched her walk away. He was filled with a feeling of apprehension. He didn't trust Donald Bancroft one bit. In fact, he had his suspicions about how Ellen had died, but the doctor had said it was a heart attack and there were no signs of any foul play so he had just had to accept the verdict. He knew Daniel to be a ruthless man though and not someone to be trusted and he would try to keep an eye on him, though quite how he did not know. Just to advise Sally when he could, he supposed, would have to do. He was so pleased that Ellen had not left Donald the house. She obviously hadn't trusted him either. He still had this awful feeling that Sally could be in danger but his hands were tied. He did hold confidences and just wished he could disclose all he knew but it wasn't his place to do so.

***

As Sally opened the front door her mother stepped over the threshold with mixed feelings. She remembered her former visit here many years ago but somehow had to convince Sally that this was her first time. Unless she could think of a good reason for their visit she wouldn't mention it unless Sally brought the subject up. Unfortunately Sally did and her mother tried to sound convincing.

"You must have imagined it, darling. We have never been here before."

Sally sighed in exasperation.

"Oh, well, if you say so. Perhaps I dreamed it. Maybe I read of the town in a book or something. It just seems such a coincidence. And I still don't know why I was left the house. I had a visit from some man called Donald who apparently is Ellen Bancroft's grandson. He made me feel really awkward. I asked Mr Underwood but he says he can't tell me anything. Though he did sort of hint that there is something he knows.

"I shouldn't worry about it, dear. Just enjoy your good fortune. I don't suppose we'll ever solve the mystery."

Sally proudly showed her mother round the house and when they reached the box room she shivered slightly and hesitated in the doorway. Her mother noticed and said "What's the matter?"

"I don't know. I just get a funny feeling about this room. When I was up with Joe sorting it out it wasn't so bad. But I don't like being up here on my own. I thought I heard noises the other day and daren't come up to investigate."

Her mother laughed. "Come on, you silly old thing. Let's go down. I want to see the garden. And I could do with a cup of tea"

Sally got out the china cups and saucers and put them on the tray along with some biscuits and set them on the table in the dining room and when they had drunk their tea they wandered around the garden strolling on the narrow paths that ran through it, taking in the trees that were all in new leaf. Daffodils and multi-coloured crocuses were just going over in the borders and some of the bluebells were showing blue through the buds along the shaded side by the wall. The blossom on the huge cherry tree was just coming into bud. The whole garden was enclosed by a brick wall and there was a wonderful sense of peace, the only sound coming from a blackbird perched on one of the branches of the apple tree.

Then Sally remembered the doll's house.

"There's something I must show you."

They re-entered the house by a side door situated up some stone steps which took them halfway up the first flight of stairs and Sally led the way into the dining room. She lifted the doll's house onto the table and carried the box of furniture and accessories from the corner of the room.

"Look, Mum, the pieces are all exact replicas of the furniture in this house. They are so beautifully made. You can help me put them into place."

So between them they took each tiny piece of furniture from it's wrapping and placed in in the appropriate room. Each bed, each wardrobe, every table and chair was put in the right place until the whole house looked identical to the one they were standing in. As they worked they lost complete track of the time and before they knew it Joe was coming in the front door, hungry for his dinner.

Sally flung herself into his arms. "Oh, Joe I'm so sorry. The dinner won't take long. I've got some lovely pasties from the shop in the town. I'll soon heat them up."

When they had eaten their hastily prepared dinner, Joe offered to wash up whilst the women went back to the doll's house to add the finishing touches to the rooms. It was then that, in the corner of the box, Sally found the tiny cheval mirror and as she unwrapped it from the tissue paper she gasped in wonderment. It was so beautiful and so perfectly made.

"I wonder where this goes. I haven't seen the real thing anywhere."

Her mother took it from her.

"I would think it is somewhere around. Everything else is here. Unless it got broken and has been thrown away. You say there are some pieces still in the box room? Perhaps it's there."

"It could be. There are some things still round the corner at the far end. I'll have a look tomorrow." She added with a laugh "If you'll come in there with me."

The next morning they were up early and after seeing Joe off to work they sat over another cup of tea. Sally loved having her mother there with her. They had always had a good relationship and she had missed her when she and her father had moved up to Yorkshire.

"You must bring Dad with you next time. I want him to see the house."

"I'll do that, dear. As soon as he can get some time off."

As they were clearing out the grates to prepare new fires to be lit, for the air was still quite chill, there was a muffled sound of footsteps coming from above. Both froze in their tracks and looked at one another.

Sally spoke first. "You see. I told you there were sounds from upstairs the other day. You heard them too, didn't you?"

Her mother seemed unable to speak for a few seconds and when she did said "Yes, darling. I heard them. What shall we do?"

"We'll grab the poker and go and have a look. After you, Mum."

9

1909

Daniel kicked out at the cat as he walked down the garden path. He had to take it out on someone and like all bullies chose someone or something smaller who couldn't fight back.

A few days earlier he had been caught out for putting Susannah's pet mouse in the oven. Oh, he hadn't meant to cook it or anything like that. He just thought it a good place to hide it. He was just fed up with Susannah going on about it as she was always going on about her pets. She never had time to spend with him. Not that he really wanted to spend time with her. He just liked to prove himself and show her that he was superior, being a boy, of course. He only wanted her company because he was short of friends.

How was he to know that his mother was going to light the oven and when she went to do so the unfortunate mouse would leap out eager to escape? His mother had very nearly fainted and had to be brought around with smelling salts.

And so he had been punished by having to stay in his room and missing a party that he had been invited to. He would get his own back on that horrible little sister of his.

At the bottom of the garden was a rope swing with a wooden seat that his father had hung from a tall fir tree and as he climbed onto it and started to swing he noticed a spider crawling up the rope. That gave him an idea. He knew his sister was terrified of spiders. He could never understand why, but it was probably because of his mother's fear of them. Apparently, they had been told, she had disturbed a nest of them in the shed when younger and had never got over the experience of them crawling up her arm.

For the whole of the next week he had been out early in the garden searching for any he could find. The old shed was an ideal place to look for them. Now he had about thirty, all sizes. A couple of them were really black with thick legs. As he watched they clambered over each other in the box - a tangled black mass.

Susannah knelt down by her doll's house. She had just put the finishing touches to a bed cover made from pieces of material her mother had given her. The tiny stitching was perfect and almost invisible. She had spent a long time on it and her fingers had been quite sore by the time it had been completed. She was now eager to put in on the bed.

As she opened the front of the house the scream that emitted from her lips penetrated the air and seemed to fill every space. Her mother came running in and really did faint this time. They were everywhere, scurrying across the floor and onto Susannah's skirt, the darkness of their legs contrasting with the pale fabric. Daniel felt the punishment he received this time was well worth it, though he did have a sore bottom for a few days.

As for the doll's house, it stood untouched. His sister could not bring herself to open it again. After three months it was decided it would be put up in the box room until she wanted to play with it again. She never did. So each tiny piece of furniture was lovingly wrapped in tissue paper by her mother and then it was carried upstairs by her father to be placed in the long room at the top of the house. This was where it would stay for over fifty years.

10

1964

As Sally and her mother walked slowly up the top flight of stairs they could still hear muffled sounds as though someone was walking about in the box room.

Apprehension engulfed Sally as she slowly clasped her fingers around the door handle and turned it. When the door opened and they peered inside it was hard to adjust to the dim light. The room was quite dark as the tiny window gave very little relief from the gloom. She flicked the switch and the room was lit up casting shadows over the remaining pieces of furniture. Boxes were still stacked along the sides. They tentatively entered and peered around, feeling rather foolish. Their hearts were pounding. There was no-one there. But still the sounds reached their ears. Now the footsteps were joined by another sound - as though some-one was moving something. The two women, then skirting round a chair with a large box on it, froze for a few seconds then walked on round the corner. They stared in disbelief when they saw a sheet moving in the corner of the room as though someone was tugging at it. Both ready to flee the room, they stood, then suddenly felt a warmth, as though some-one had switched on an electric heater. Their fear evaporated as though by magic.

As Sally reached out and gently lifted the sheet she saw it. It was the cheval mirror that had been copied for the doll's house and it was beautiful. The noises had stopped. There was complete silence. Even the sounds of their breathing had ceased. They realised then that they were both holding their breath.

"Well, we've found the mirror. What do you think we should do with it."

Sally did not hesitate before answering. "I shall put it in my bedroom. I'm sure that is where it is meant to be."

Her mother helped her lift the mirror from it's hiding place.

"I have never believed in ghosts but now I'm beginning to think again. Someone wanted us to bring this mirror downstairs and put it back where it belongs."

They carefully carried it down the stairs and placed it in the room where Ellen had once slept. As they uncovered it they heard, what seemed to them, a sigh of relief. Turning to leave the room they did not notice the reflection that watched them. It was a child in a green party dress with ringlets in her hair.

11

September 1919

Ellen stood in front of the cheval mirror and surveyed her reflection. She was lucky to have kept her trim figure and the person looking back at her was extremely attractive. She was wearing a pale green silk dress that fell in soft folds around her ankles. On the bodice was embroidery enhanced by pearls. The colour emphasised her dark auburn hair, in which was placed a small bunch of feathers, that matched her dress perfectly and were held together with a diamante clip. She was not yet forty and although she considered her daughter a little too young to be getting married, she was pleased that she herself was still young enough to look good.

Life had been kind to Ellen. She had a happy and fulfilling marriage and the only sadness she had encountered was when her dear brother was killed on the Somme. He had enlisted at the beginning of the war and quickly worked his way up to Sergeant. He had died alongside many of his comrades, in the filth and mud of the trenches. The war had taken it's toll on many a family but Ellen was thankful that Daniel had still been too young when other sons were being conscripted into the forces. Many friends had lost their sons in the terrible carnage and she thanked God that her son was safe as the war had now come to an end. It had not been 'over by Christmas' as many had predicted but had lasted for more than four terrible years.

Even the dreadful influenza, that had struck down so many in 1918, had not touched Ellen's family.

Susannah had known David since their school days and Ellen was delighted to welcome him into the family. His mother and father had been friends with Ellen and William for a long time.

Ellen turned to look out of the window. It was promising to be a fine day. The garden was bathed in sunshine and was still looking colourful with late summer flowers. Most of the roses were still in full bloom and some rambled over the walls and fruit trees which were laden with apples and pears. Victoria plums had been picked and placed in the large fruit bowl on the dining room table.

The wedding was to take place at St. Mary's Church and the reception at The Cock Hotel in the High Street. Nothing had been spared to make this a day to remember.

There were to be three small bridesmaids in lemon and Susannah's best friend, Ruth, was matron-of-honour.

As Ellen stood gazing out onto the garden there was an excited knock at the door and before waiting for an answer three little faces peered round it followed by three lemon figures each tumbling over one another to get into the room.

"Please" they chorused in union "may we look in your mirror?"

Ellen laughed and stepped back so that they were in full view. "Of course you may. My, you look beautiful, all of you."

The girls twirled and primped as they looked at themselves. The dresses had minute bows all down the front and the hems were looped up to show frilly petticoats and pantaloons beneath. On their feet were pure white satin slippers. Their heads were adorned with wreaths of tiny lemon and white rosebuds and in their hands they carried small baskets holding matching flowers with ribbons trailing from them.

There was another knock at the door and Susannah entered looking a dream, her mother thought, in cream lace. Her hair hung in tendrils around her face and was topped with a wreath of lemon roses, which, though larger, matched the ones the small bridesmaids carried. Ellen loved this daughter of hers and felt such pride in how she looked. She led her to the mirror and stood looking over her shoulder, her arm about her daughter's waist. A smile touched her lips.

The whole day went off perfectly and at the end of it husband and wife waved to all as they drove off in a large black Austin car to their honeymoon on the south coast.

When they returned two weeks later Ellen had arranged for a photographer to come to the house to take some formal wedding photographs of the happy couple. So the little bridesmaids once again donned their finery along with Ruth and Ellen to capture the memories of the day.

12

1964

Sally had lost her fear of the box room so decided it was time she delved further into what it held. There were still several boxes and trunks to open.

The fear of getting shut in still lingered though, as there was no window within reach, so she propped the door open with a large box as she entered.

As she went further in she was not sure what to do first. Her eyes went to a large trunk and she decided this was where she would start. The lid was extremely heavy but, once she managed to lift it, let out a gasp. Beneath the layers of tissue paper lay the most exquisite dresses. As she withdrew them one at a time she found she was holding her breath. She spread a sheet on a chair nearby to lay them out on. A delicate smell of roses reached her nostrils as she took the first one from the trunk. She knew it must have been the perfume worn so many years before and wondered how the smell had survived all this time.

The first dress she lifted out to lay on the chair was of pale green silk which was as light as swansdown and then, as she thought it couldn't get any better, lifted another layer of tissue to reveal a dress in cream lace. It was obviously a wedding dress and there were even a few paper rose petals clinging to the bodice. She held it against her and stroked the exquisite fabric. How she wished she could have worn this at her own wedding. She had begun to think that she would never wear a nice dress ever again. She always seemed to be dressed in baggy trousers and jumpers nowadays. But then, where did she go to wear anything slightly attractive. She spent all her time poking around in corners of rooms.

Just as she was about to replace the dresses in the trunk she noticed a book covered in fine green leather and on opening it saw the photographs.

She took the book downstairs to peruse over whilst she had a cup of coffee. The kettle was singing on the range, so she lifted it and poured hot water onto the instant coffee granules in the mug and took a couple of biscuits out of the biscuit barrel.

Seating herself at the pine table she opened the book. There were numerous photographs staring back at her. They were in sepia and looked very old. Of course she didn't know the people so skipped over several pages until she came to three photographs of a wedding.

She knew immediately that the dresses being worn were the same ones she had found in the trunk. This straight away held her interest and she looked at the people standing wooden-like in poses where they were not allowed to move for a whole minute. She thought how hard that must have been. No wonder the smiles on their faces looked as though they had been painted on.

All of a sudden, as she looked at the bride's face she felt a sense of recognition. She was sure she had seen this person before. She looked so familiar. It was quite uncanny. She opened the dresser drawer and withdrew a magnifying glass to get a closer look. Yes, she had definitely seen this person before. But where?

When Joe came home that evening she showed him her find. He tried for her sake to show some interest but could not connect with these people whom he had never known. He did, however, agree with Sally that the bride looked very familiar.

13

1919

David and Susannah rented a house in Verulam Road not far from where she had been brought up. It was a quiet road and though the house was not large it was very cosy and she found great pleasure in choosing furniture, carpets and drapes. It was of a manageable size and even had the latest electric lights installed in place of the gas lamps.

Ellen was most impressed when visiting her and decided to persuade William to have electricity put in their house. To get light at the touch of a switch seemed magical and, for more than half an hour, she wandered around Susannah's rooms just to turn the lights on and off.

Within the year her request was carried out. This was done at the cost of great chaos. Floor boards had to be taken up, ceilings taken down and everywhere was covered with a layer of dust whilst work was in progress. It took all of six weeks, but at the end of it Ellen considered it worth every inconvenience they had suffered. Lights shone from every corner of the house.

Susannah gave birth to a girl just a year after they were married and Ellen adored her from the very start. She was there at the birth and had been the first to hold the baby in her arms. There was to grow a deep bond between them.

The baby was christened at St Mary's Church, where her parents had been wed. She was named Patricia Ellen.

Ellen was there through her babyhood and formative years and when she started school was usually at her daughter's side whenever they watched a concert or play. Patricia was a lovable child and had an abundance of friends. She was always being invited to parties.

It was not so with her grandson Donald, Daniel's son. For some unknown reason his friendships never seemed to last. He was not a likeable child and Ellen always felt a stab of guilt when she thought of how much she loved Patricia. She couldn't quite put her finger on it but there seemed to be something sneaky about Donald. He would never quite look you in the eye and his gaze would shift around to avoid doing so.

Daniel had clung to his freedom for as long as possible but had at last succumbed to marriage. His wife, Alice, was the daughter of an important lawyer in the town, and although there was no love on his side he considered the marriage was a good move. She was a quiet girl and a dutiful daughter. Daniel liked these qualities. She would be easy to manipulate.

He had always been a selfish child and this did not change when he became a man, putting his own pleasures before anyone else's and this trait seemed even more prominent with him getting a wife. Many a time Ellen had to bite her tongue not to reprimand him as she had done when he was a child. She knew it was not her place to do so, though found it very hard. He treated Alice as though she was his servant and had been put on this earth just to please him. Ellen felt that, perhaps, it was her fault that Daniel had turned out as he was and because of this became very close to Alice, trying to help her in any small way she could.

This was even more so when Alice gave birth to their son, Donald. He was not an easy baby and seemed to take after his father in wanting every moment of Alice's time and attention. She was at his beck and call every moment of the day and he had not improved when going through the toddling stage.

When Alice visited Ellen she could see how worn out her daughter-in-law was. She had lost a lot of weight and her clothes seemed to hang on her.

"Why don't you come and stay for a while? I'll help you look after Donald and you could get a bit of your strength back."

Alice knew without doubt that it was just what she needed - to be cared for and pampered as she knew only Ellen would do. The offer was not met with the same enthusiasm by Daniel. He did not wish to be beholden to his mother in any way. This was possibly because his mother understood him a little too well. He could never pull the wool over her eyes.

However, despite Daniel's protestations, Ellen got her own way and mother and child were installed in the back bedroom. Daniel insisted on staying in his own home, which Ellen was rather pleased about.

She threw herself wholeheartedly into giving her daughter-in-law every comfort and took great pleasure in watching her being transformed. Gone was her haggard look and, as flesh began to fill out her face, her eyes regained their old sparkle.

During these few weeks that Ellen cared for Alice she grew even closer to her granddaughter. Patricia proved to be quite an asset when caring for Donald. She loved playing the little mother and would tend to his needs and demands. These were many. He seemed to feel it his right to be pampered and these traits were to develop into major difficulties as he grew older. He would stamp his foot and shout in protest should he be thwarted in any way.

14

1964

Donald was doing everything in his power to wheedle his way into Sally and Joe's life. He would call at the house on any pretext, often bringing a bunch of flowers or chocolates hoping to impress Sally. He often made the excuse that there something about the house that they should know from damp areas, smoking chimneys, the well in the garden and even to warn them about their neighbours. Sally was not taken in by his efforts. In fact, she rather liked their neighbours. She still did not trust Donald and felt uneasy in his presence.

He was not invited to come in at any time. Sally always made the excuse that she was going out. It even got to the point where she would have a hat handy to slip on in case it was him whenever there was a knock at the door. She thought this rather funny because normally she would not wear a hat.

It was around this time that she started to have strange feelings about the mirror. Often, when she walked past it she thought she caught a glimpse of someone reflected in it - some movement - and had quickly looked round fully expecting to see another person standing there. This happened several times and made her feel uneasy. She decided she would put it back up in the box room.

Joe didn't comment on her decision, in fact didn't even notice it was gone until she told him three days later. He spent little time in the bedroom except when in bed and quickly getting dressed in the mornings. He wasn't a vain person and rarely looked in a mirror.

Then the noises started again. They came from the box room as before. She felt the hair stand on end as she sat on the stairs wondering what she should do. She decided to ignore them for a few days but they just got worse. Joe laughed when she told him.

"You've got such an imagination, darling."

The sounds just got louder and she knew she had got to prove a point so she very bravely went up into box room and brought the mirror down placing it back in the bedroom. The noises stopped immediately.

She remembered the saying 'if you can't beat them join them' and decided to leave the mirror where it was and try to come to terms with it.

The evenings were drawing in now it was October and Sally thankfully drew the curtains across to shut out the gloom. As she lit the bedside lamp she caught a glimpse of something moving and realised it was a reflection in the mirror. She lowered herself on to the bed and sitting quietly she looked at the mirror and relaxed. After only a few moments she felt a chill in the room. A cold draft seemed to wash over her and she shivered. Then her skin turned icy cold with goose-bumps for as she looked into the mirror a mist clouded it. Then the mist cleared and she saw the reflection of a girl in a pink and white robe. She closed her eyes and when she opened them again the girl was gone. Strangely she now felt no fear. There was a comfortable warmth wrapping itself around her body.

She concentrated hard as she stared at the mirror and saw to her amazement that the figure had re-appeared. It hovered for a few seconds then disappeared from view.

This became a regular event in her everyday life. She did not tell Joe, knowing he would only laugh at her. But each day she would sit on the bed and just stare into the mirror. The mist would form and images would flit across the glass. Faces and figures would appear, each one for only a matter of seconds. Colours would mingle with the mist and drift in and out of her line of vision. She felt a great sense of peace when this was happening. It was also frustrating for her as she felt she was trying to catch a beautiful butterfly that would not stay still long enough.

15

Summer 1938

When Ellen answered the ring of the door bell, she did not at once recognise the man on the door step although he seemed vaguely familiar. He was dressed all in black, wearing a heavy coat that was at odds with the weather as the sun was streaming down on this warm August day. His face held a strained, worried expression and his eyes seemed far too large for his face.

Then, as he spoke her name and she heard the German accent she realised it was an old friend of William's whom she had met only a couple of times. She tried to recall his name but could not and felt rather ill at ease.

He smiled and relieved the tension. The smile seemed to shed years off his age.

"I'm Bernard Goldstein. Perhaps you don't remember me."

Ellen immediately smiled and held out her hand.

"Of course. Please forgive me. I did recognise you but could not think where we had met. Do come in."

She ushered him through the front door and indicated for him to go into the lounge. He sank thankfully into an armchair.

"I'm afraid William is not here at the moment. He is at the printing works."

The man had removed his hat and laid it on a side table. He looked a little uncomfortable.

"No, please not to worry. I did not really expect him to be in at this time of the day. I can come back later - only I have just got off the train and wanted to be sure I had got the right address."

Although he spoke with a German accent his English was impeccable.

"No, please do stay. William should be home within the hour. He usually comes home for a bite of lunch. You are welcome to join us."

The man smiled for the second time, though Ellen couldn't help but feel this was a rare occurrence.

"That is very kind of you. If it is not too much trouble I would like that very much. Please don't go to any trouble though. A sandwich would be fine.

"It's no trouble I assure you. We always have a light snack at midday. I know William will be really pleased to see you."

"Thank you. You are very kind."

"That's settled then. Let me take your coat."

At this a look of alarm spread over his face.

"No, no, I will keep it on if I may."

Ellen stared at him and could not hide the surprise on her face. How strange not to remove his coat on such a warm day - and indoors at that.

" Would you like a cup of tea whilst you are waiting? Or perhaps something a little stronger?"

" A cup of tea would be most welcome. Thank you."

When she returned it was with a tray on which stood a pot of tea, two china cups and saucers and some home made biscuits.

He seemed reluctant to talk so she did not press him and they drank in silence, Ellen feeling very uncomfortable. She was not used to keeping quiet so long and tried to make conversation. She was glad when they had, at last, emptied their cups and asked him if he would like to stroll round the garden.

"Oh, I would love to, if you don't mind. I love English gardens. There are none like them in the whole world."

Ellen felt very proud of the garden as she showed him out of the side door and proceeded down the stone steps. She sensed he wanted to be alone so did not offer to accompany him but walked back up the stairs so that she could watch him from the window as he wandered amongst the trees and along the pathways. He would stop every now and then to put his nose to the roses and breath in deeply, savouring the scent. There was a terrible sense of sadness about him and it relayed itself to Ellen. It brought tears to her eyes. Whatever was it that was making him so sad?

When William arrived home for his lunch he was delighted to see his old friend and they went into the dining room to talk whilst Ellen prepared a light meal of ham and salad. She had baked bread earlier that day and now cut some and placed it on a side plate with pats of butter. As she entered the dining room she got the feeling that Bernard wanted to talk to William in private so she left them to eat alone.

It was only now that Bernard took off his coat but he was reluctant to part with it and held it close to him.

William and Bernard had met when they were both at an Oxford University and they had hit if off immediately. They had shared the same passions and beliefs and would sit well into the early hours of the morning discussing every issue they could think of. They had played rugby and cricket together, both representing university teams in local matches.

It was obvious to everyone that Bernard was Jewish because of his name and looks and even all those years ago there were some who would not accept him. It had been repeated through the ages and it was taking a long time to change opinions. William had often ruminated over the plight of his friend and wished it could have been different but wondered if it would ever be so.

But, despite their differences, they had remained friends and although Bernard had returned to his native country of Germany they had kept in touch and met up when he had been in England, usually for a day spent in London. He owned a jewellery shop in Berlin which he had inherited from his father and was quite a wealthy man, though William did not know how wealthy. It was not something they spoke of.

Now, as he sat with his old friend, William could sense that something was wrong. He had to return to the printers, which he ran with a partner, quite soon as they had a minor crisis on their hands but asked Bernard if he would like to stay with them for the night. He hadn't asked Ellen but knew she would not object. The reward was the pleasure that showed on Bernard's face as he replied.

"Oh, thank you so much. I knew I could rely on my old friend. I have so much to tell you."

After lunch when William had returned to work Ellen made up a bed with clean sheets and showed Bernard up to the room. He lay on the bed and fell asleep. She looked in on him several times but he had not even changed position so she left him in peace and did not wake him until William was due home again. He looked more refreshed as he came down the stairs and seemed a lot more at ease, though he still carried his coat with him.

Early evening they had eaten their fill of a delicious dinner cooked by Ellen, of roast chicken and small roast potatoes. She had picked runner beans from the garden.

She served them coffee and left them to their conversation. Now they sat in the lounge. Though it was still summer it had grown chill and William had lit a fire to give a glow to the room. He had opened a bottle of his favourite whiskey and they toasted each other. Then William was glad of the warmth of the fire and the alcohol as his blood ran cold digesting the facts that Bernard was relating to him. He told how the

Jews were being persecuted in Berlin and how a lot had been forced to leave their homes. Any possessions of value were confiscated.

He had had to leave his dear wife, Rachel, there whilst he travelled to England on this important mission and was longing to get back to her as she was so afraid. He was going to go back and see what they could salvage.

He then asked William if Ellen had a pair of nail scissors he could use. Mystified, William went to her bedroom to ask where she kept them and after going to her workbox he took them out and went back into the lounge where Bernard was clutching his coat.

When William handed him the tiny scissors he took them in his large fingers, spread the coat over his lap and began to snip at the seams in the lining.

William watched in complete amazement as one by one he undid a few stitches and extracted tiny diamonds. Neither man spoke and when Bernard had finished snipping and pulling there lay on the table more than a hundred. They each caught the light from the numerous lamps that were placed around the room and were breathtaking.

"I want you to look after these for me, my dear friend. If I ever get out of this terrible situation I will come back for them. And if I do not" he hesitated and his eyes met William's "they are yours."

"But they must be worth a fortune. You must keep them."

"If I keep them they will be taken from me as soon as I return home. We are not allowed to keep anything of value. Everything is confiscated by the Nazis. No, William. You must keep them safe. You are the only person I can trust."

16

September 1939

The family sat in silence as they listened to Neville Chamberlain's sombre voice on the radio. No-one was surprised at the news that they were now at war with Germany. It had been expected but, nevertheless, it still hit hard. No-one spoke for a full ten minutes. They all just sat, each thinking how this would change their lives.

For months now everyone had hoped and prayed that it would not come to this but each in their own way had known in their hearts that it had been inevitable. Hitler's invasions could not go unheeded.

Ellen looked across at William and could see the strain showing on his face. They had been through one war together and though they had come through it virtually unscathed, except for the loss of Samuel, they knew they had been lucky. This time it would be different. Although there was a chance that Daniel may not be called up to enlist they had a grandson who was at the age to fight.

She also knew he was thinking of his friend, Bernard. They had not heard from him since April, and even then had only received a short letter saying things were not too good, and both feared for his safety. It appeared that the letter had been censored which was not a good sign.

Patricia also listened with a heavy heart. She had recently become engaged to Alec Linden and they had planned to marry in the Spring but she knew he would volunteer to go in the Army. He had mentioned it several times. She had tried to talk him out of it and persuade him to wait until he was called up but he was determined to go as soon as possible.

"The sooner we get in there, the sooner we will beat the bastards and get out again." he said, with great conviction in his voice.

Donald, on the other hand was not quite so sure. He was not ready to put his life on the line. Like his father before him he had always been a coward.

As his father had bullied Susannah when she was young he had carried on the tradition and did his best to keep Patricia under his thumb.

During their childhood years he had ruled her. She was a likeable and biddable child and was always everyone's favourite. This had annoyed him intensely and at every opportunity he had belittled her and spoilt her fun.

Perhaps it had been due to him that she now had such a strong character for, as they reached their late teen years, she had started to retaliate and become stronger whilst he had become the weaker of the two.

Ellen had watched them with interest as they had grown up but her reluctance to intervene had probably helped Patricia for now she stood up to Donald in her own right.

***

Because Hitchin was relatively safe from bombing, evacuees began to arrive in the town. When Ellen heard that homes were needed for them she did not hesitate but went with Susannah to the station to welcome them and as they lined the platform waiting for the train to arrive from King's Cross they felt a sense of apprehension. Neither spoke but stood in silence, lost in their own thoughts. No-one knew what to expect.

The train eventually pulled in, having been held up at Stevenage, where several evacuees had already disembarked. There was a sea of frightened faces peering from the windows and as the children were ushered on to the platform those who had siblings with them clung onto them for fear that if they let go they would lose them and never see them again. The older children, though little bigger than their younger brothers and sisters, instinctively tried to take charge and protect them; though against what, they knew not.

Susannah's eyes were immediately drawn to a small boy with the biggest, saddest eyes she had ever seen. She surmised that he was about six years old and was clinging to a slightly older girl and trying to hide behind her skirt. Each had the obligatory box around their neck containing their gas masks and on their jackets were pinned labels on which were written their names. She nudged her mother and signalled for her to follow, which she did.

She bent down to the little boy and read out loud "John Turnbull, why that's a grand name."

He gulped between sobs "My Mummy calls me Johnny."

The girl, who was obviously his sister as her name read 'Betty Turnbull' bent down to wipe his tears away with a piece of rag which she extracted from her pocket.

Johnny's blonde hair tumbled over his forehead, mingling with his tears and Betty was trying to push it back so he could see. The first stop would be the barbers, Ellen thought, after they had given the hair a good wash as it was highly probable it would have some unwelcome visitors in it. Betty's was tied back with a badly frayed piece of ribbon and could also do with a good wash.

Both Ellen's and Susannah's hearts went out to them and they had no hesitation in signing the obligatory piece of paper that the stout lady in charge held out to them and once addresses had been exchanged mother and daughter made their way out of the station and proceeded to walk along the road to their home. Johnny was clutching Betty's hand for dear life. Because he was so thin his short trousers had to be hitched up every couple of minutes, only to slip straight down again. His socks also gravitated towards the ground and ended up in wrinkles around his ankles.

When they reached the house Ellen poured them both a glass of milk and handed them a biscuit. Johnny was still clinging onto his sister but his sobs had subsided and when he saw the biscuit he nearly smiled.

The next thing Ellen did was to run them a nice warm bath and called for Susannah to bring them up to the bathroom. As they entered it their eyes were like saucers. They had never seen a real bath before. At home they had the tin bath in front of the fire - that was when they had enough coal to light a fire, which wasn't very often. Ellen and Susannah lifted the children into the warm water. It was a only a few inches deep as there were restrictions in place over how much water one was allowed to use and the children smiled at each other as they sat down. They stayed in there for over a half an hour, long after the water had grown chill.

Then it was in front of a blazing fire with a cup of Ovaltine each. There faces were a joy to watch. For a short while the two children forgot their sadness at leaving their home and mother. It wasn't until they were tucked up in bed when it returned. They wanted their mother to kiss them goodnight as she had done every night of their short lives.

Susannah held Johnny as he sobbed and as tiredness overtook him she gently laid him back on the pillow. Her heart ached for him. He was only six years old and been wrenched away from his mother and home.

Betty was trying her hardest to be brave for his sake but once he was asleep she let the tears stream down her face. Susannah wiped them away.

"It'll be better in the morning. Just you see."

Back in London the sadness was ten fold as their mother stood looking down at their empty beds. Her husband was away fighting and she was completely alone.

Patricia was right about Alec. No matter how much she tried to persuade him to wait he went almost immediately to the Recruitment Office to sign on. To placate Patricia he suggested they get married straight away so that they could at least spend some time together before he had to go for training,

The wedding was a very quiet affair. It was held in St Mary's Church, as her mother's had been, but with none of the trimmings of the one she had planned. At least they managed to get a honeymoon in, albeit only a few days in Norfolk at his aunt's home. She made them very welcome but already they could see the preparations being put in action for prevention of attack from the sea. Pill boxes were being erected as lookout points and rolls of barbed wire were waiting to be put up. There was hardly any beach to walk on and though they tried hard not to dwell on the war as it was their honeymoon they found it almost impossible to put it out of their minds with all the reminders around them. It was not a happy few days and they were relieved to be back home again.

Although they had planned to rent a house, Patricia gratefully took up her grandmother's offer of them living with her. She knew Alec would be away most of the time and she had no wish to be alone. Also her mother lived round the corner so she would be able to visit often.

Her grandmother was thrilled to have her living at the house. They shared every pleasure that was possible in these hard times and the presence of Johnny and Betty helped enormously. They was a constant source of interest. Every experience they encountered was new to them from their play in the garden and the odd trip to the cinema. Ellen and Patricia often wondered how they had survived before the children came. They had not realised just how empty the house had been.

William had bought the children a pet rabbit each and the look on their faces when he put them in the hastily prepared hutch was a joy to behold.

17

December 1939

They all knew that Christmas would not be the same this year with the threat of bombs hanging over everyone and the shortages beginning to bite. But all the same they wanted it to be special for the children.

Betty and Johnny had been with them for three months and Ellen recalled how hard it had been for them at first.

She had put them both in the same bedroom and each had their own little bed but inevitably each morning she would find them snuggled up together, Betty with her arm protectively round her brother. When she passed their room at night she would hear Johnny's soft crying and Betty muttering comforting words to him. During the day he spoke very little, only answering the most necessary questions. She knew he missed his mother dreadfully.

They had been accepted into St Saviours, a school just two roads away and they went quite happily every morning, Johnny clinging to Betty's hand. In his other hand he held the penny Ellen had given him to spend and they would stop at The Cabin, the little shop they passed on the way, to buy a currant bun.

The turning point in Johnny's life came on a Sunday afternoon when Ellen had suggested they all go to the Bancroft Recreation Ground to hear the band play. The children were quite excited and wearing their new Sunday-best clothes that Ellen had bought for them walked hand in hand down Verulam road, chatting together. It was quite chilly, being mid-October and they were well wrapped in scarves and gloves. They turned into the gate that led past the putting green edged with flower beds and reached the place where the stout, upright lady, wearing a large blue felt hat, was collecting the money. Ellen put tuppence into each of their hands and they proudly handed it over. On the bandstand the men were already tuning up. Ellen, Susannah, Betty and Johnny sat on the chairs that had been set out in rows.

Ellen told the children that whilst they were waiting for it to start, if they wished, they could run around on the small paths that ran between

the flower beds. Betty went to take Johnny's hand to lead him away but he shrugged her hand away and just sat, his eyes glued on the red uniforms of the bandsmen. On their head they wore smart peaked caps.

The younger bandsmen were all serving in the forces and the ones that were left had mostly come out of retirement to keep the band going. They had squeezed into uniforms that had long been outgrown and definitely seen better days. But they taken their places with pride. Their instruments shone with the loving care each one had been given and reflected the autumn sunlight. They were all accomplished musicians and the sounds that emitted from the brass instruments rose to a crescendo on the autumn air. As soon as they had begun to play Johnny was enthralled. He had never heard a brass band before and just sat with his mouth open. Ellen looked at him and smiled. His little face was so lit up she watched him more than she did the band. It was such a sight. Then she remembered something.

As they reached home and took off their coats she made her way straight up to the box room. Opening a large trunk she found what she was looking for and carried it down to Johnny. When she offered it to him a large grin lit up his whole face. Except for the incident on the day of his arrival when he had been put in the bath and when he had been given the rabbit this was the first time she had really seen him smile.

He put the little trumpet to his lips and blew with all his might. It was a very strange sound that emerged and they all laughed. From that moment he became a different boy. The trumpet was never out of his sight when he was home. He would even take it to bed with him. One day she had let him take it to school to show his teacher.

As Ellen tucked them up in bed that night Betty asked "Is Bancroft Recreation Ground named after you Auntie Ellen?"

Ellen laughed. "No, my darling. Nothing so grand. I'm not sure who it's named after but it's not us."

Now Christmas was nearly upon them and Ellen was determined to make it one for them to remember. It was lovely, she thought, having young children in the house again. Christmas was just not quite the same without them.

She called for them both to come up to the box room with her and as they clambered over the various bits and pieces of discarded furniture they came to a large box and struggled back to the door with it between them. Then, with difficulty, they managed to carry it down the stairs and on reaching the lounge emptied the contents over the carpet.

The children's eyes lit up as they saw garlands and baubles of every imaginable colour tumble over the floor and in no time at all they had transformed the room into fairyland. A large Christmas tree had been placed in the corner beforehand and this they decorated until hardly a branch could be seen.

On Christmas Eve the children had the best surprise of all - one that Ellen had been saving for them. There was a ring at the doorbell and when Betty went to answer it found her mother on the door step. She stepped into her mother's arms and hugged her.

Johnny stood stock still. He was not sure about this stranger. Three months was a long time for a six-year-old. Then his mother spoke to him and suddenly he was being held as they both cried.

It was a wonderful Christmas and for a few days everyone in the house tried to forget the horrors of the war.

Because the threat of bombs had not materialised many children were returning to their families and it was arranged for Betty and Johnny to go home at the end of January but then came the news that their father had been injured so Ellen did not hesitate to say she would keep them on as long as need be. If truth be told, she was reluctant to see them go. As it turned out it was for the best, for the bombs did eventually come and London was devastated.

So the two children became a permanent part of the family.

18

April-June 1940

When Alec finally completed his training and said his goodbyes to Patricia and his family she did not know then that she was pregnant with his child. It was soon after that she started to suffer with morning sickness and went to see her doctor. She was both thrilled and scared. It was not the best time to bring a baby into the world.

Ellen was 'over the moon'. She couldn't wait to become a great grandmother. She knew it would be hard for Patricia but with her family behind her she was sure she would be alright.

Alec did not know then where he was being sent. It was to be France and he was to be one of the thousands of soldiers who were forced to retreat to Dunkirk when the Germans relentlessly pushed on through the country. Thousands were taken off the beaches to safety. He was not one of them.

Patricia answered the knock on the door to see the telegram boy holding an envelope in his hand. He looked sheepish. Some days he hated his job. He quickly handed her the envelope as though it was hot and he couldn't wait to let it go and as he walked down the steps to pick up his bicycle he heard Patricia cry out. He ran back up the steps to find her lying on the floor.

Ellen sat by the bed with Patricia's hand in hers. The doctor had been called and had given her a sedative which caused her to sleep for several hours. Now she opened her eyes and looked at the clock. At first could not recall why she was in bed in the middle of the day. Then she looked into her grandmother's kindly face which was ravaged with grief - and remembered.

Ellen spoke gently to her. "I'm so sorry, dear. You have lost the baby. But you mustn't give up hope on Alec though. It only said he was missing. He may have been taken prisoner."

Three weeks had passed and Patricia had not shed any tears. She was locked in grief and no matter what any of them tried they could not bring her out of it. The days and weeks passed by and Patricia just walked around in a trance. She not only yearned for Alec but for the baby she had lost.

Ellen's heart ached for this granddaughter whom she loved so much and she just didn't know how to help her. Had it not been wartime she would have suggested they go away together for a few days but there was really nowhere to go and they had the children to think of.

The turning point came through Johnny being very ill with diphtheria. He was taken into the isolation hospital and was allowed no visitors. Ellen was distraught. She had come to love this little boy as her own and the thought of losing him tore her apart.

Patricia forgot her own sorrow when seeing her grandmother so upset and having someone else to care about made her put it to the back of her mind.

At last Johnny made a full recovery and was allowed back home. Although he was still very weak they arranged a special tea party for him with jelly and blancmange. Betty was thrilled to have him back and made a great fuss of him.

That evening after they had tucked the children up in their beds and were sitting by the fireside listening to the wireless Patricia told them of her decision. She had decided to train as a nurse.

"I want to do my bit for the war and I think I'd be quite good at nursing."

Ellen looked quite surprised at this news, then as she thought about it agreed with her granddaughter.

"I think you would make a lovely nurse, dear. You have always been caring even when you were tiny. How will you go about it - I mean where will you train?"

"I don't really know. I'll go to the North Herts Hospital and ask there. Someone should be able to tell me what to do."

So the very next day she set off early and returned two hours later with numerous pieces of paper filled with information and a form to fill in and within two weeks was off to a training hospital in London. Nurses were desperately needed and no time was wasted in getting them trained.

19

Spring 1964

Mary Bolton had visited her daughter Sally three times and each time they had grown closer. They had always had a good relationship but now it was as if the house was weaving a spell round them. They were very relaxed in each other's company delving around in the box room and uncovering various small items, which they spread around the many rooms.

It was early June now and the garden had come into its own. There was a riot of colour and the perfume of the roses was quite heady, mingled with the lavender. At the end of the lawn a mock orange bush grew and the smell could be enjoyed as far as the back door when they first came out into the garden. The women would sniff the air appreciatively as they came out into the sunshine.

Sally had dug up a small patch of earth to plant some vegetables and suggested they go along to the market to see what they could get. She knew very little about growing vegetables but felt that with her mother's advice they could find something to plant. Mary actually thought it a bit late to think about planting vegetables but didn't want to curb her daughter's enthusiasm.

The market was bustling and they had to push their way through to the plant stall. It seemed everyone had the same idea. Sally and her mother managed to find a few that could be planted now and decided to carry them back to the house and return later for a longer look round the other stalls.

It was as they were walking back across Portmill Lane that Sally heard her name being called and on turning saw Andrew Underwood.

"You look rather laden, if I may say so."

Sally smiled at this kindly man "Yes. We are rather. I have decided to start a vegetable garden. Well, just a small one - a patch really. Oh, by the way, this is my mother. Mum, this is Mr Underwood, our solicitor."

Sally nearly dropped one of the boxes of plants and retrieving it missed the glance that passed between Andrew Underwood and her mother. He held out his hand. "It's so very nice to meet you, Mrs Bolton."

"You too, Mr Underwood. My daughter has told me how kind you have been."

The old man looked embarrassed and shook his head. "Oh, no, no, no. It's been a pleasure, I assure you. She is like a breath of fresh air in my stuffy old world. I have enjoyed every minute of it. Won't you stop by the office and partake of a cup of tea with me?"

"Thank you all the same." Sally answered " I think we had better get home with this lot before we drop them."

"Of course, of course. I do understand. Perhaps another time."

"Yes, that would be lovely. Thank you."

As the two women walked away Sally remarked. "He's such a lovely man. He lost his wife last year and I think he gets very lonely."

"Has he any family?"

"Well, he did mention a son but I believe he lives in Canada so he doesn't see much of him."

Mother and daughter spent an enjoyable afternoon in the garden and felt very pleased with their efforts when at last they went back indoors. Their backs ached slightly but after soaking in a nice hot bath they sat enjoying a cup a tea when the doorbell rang. Donald stood on the doorstep. Sally couldn't pretend she was just going out so had no choice but to ask him in. She introduced him to her mother and felt uneasy when he looked her over as though she were beneath him. The atmosphere was tense and Sally asked him what he wanted.

"I just wanted to know how you were getting on. I know it's a big house and can be rather daunting."

As Sally had been living there now for several months she thought this rather an odd comment to make and stressed when answering him how wonderful she thought it was.

"I think it's a beautiful house, Mr Bancroft, and feel very lucky to be here."

"Oh, please do call me Donald. We must be friends."

Both women sighed with relief when at last they had got rid of him.

"That man gives me the creeps" her mother said

"Yes I know what you mean. Ellen Bancroft couldn't have trusted him if she ordered him from the house. I wonder why."

When her mother had left to return home Sally felt at a loss. She missed her company. To give herself something to do she went again to the box room to see what else she could unearth. What she did find gave her a thrill of excitement. When delving into a deep box her hand touched upon a journal which she guessed had been written in Ellen

Bancroft's hand. It was in a beautiful slanted script. She carefully took it downstairs to read.

Inside the cover were the words *To our dear daughter, Ellen, on her 16th birthday. August 30th 1898 so she can recall all her most precious moments.*

On the first page was written *Today is my sixteenth birthday and I am so happy. I have had a wonderful party with six of my friends and so many wonderful gifts. My favourite one is my cheval mirror which Mother and Father gave me. It will take pride of place in my bedroom.*

Sally read on through Ellen's memories. Besides all the day to day trivial things which a young girl had written she read of how Will had come into her life, of their marriage and the births of Daniel and Susannah. At first she felt as though she was spying but after a while she become completely absorbed in Ellen's life. This first journal ended in 1910 so Sally carefully put it back in its tissue wrapping and ran up stairs to find the next one. It was in the box where she had found the first. She couldn't wait to read it but knew she must do some housework and then go shopping so set about her chores.

On the way to the shops she bumped into Mr Underwood and he asked after her mother.

"Oh, she's fine, thank you. She so enjoyed her visit. I hope she'll be back in the summer."

She hurried home, picked up the journal and carried it into the garden. A breeze had blown up but she found a sheltered spot and placing her chair there, the journal on her lap, she settled down to read..

There was quite a lot written about the children's early years. The episode of the doll's house was recorded. *I was so cross with Daniel today. He put spiders in Susannah's doll's house and frightened her very badly. He frightened me too and I fainted. He knows how I hate spiders. I cannot forgive him. I worry about him sometimes. He can be quite vindictive and has a nasty streak.*

On September 3rd 1939 the entry read *Today we are all so sad and worried. We are at war with Germany. William is very concerned over his friend Bernard and what he has entrusted us with. It is such a big responsibility. I know I cannot write anymore but just feel I need to tell someone. I hope and pray that Bernard comes back safely.*

That evening after they had worked in the garden for a couple of hours Sally showed Joe the entry.

"I wonder what it was. It's a mystery."

"Well, I don't think we'll ever find out. It was a long time ago. Come on, let's get to bed. I've got an early start in the morning.

Sally felt sad when she picked up the journal the next day and read the entry saying *"Today I have said goodbye to my dear granddaughter. She has left us to start her nurse's training in London. I pray to God to keep her safe until she comes home again. I will miss her so much.*

This is a terrible war. So many of our young boys have gone. I pray that it will soon be over so we can all return to normal."

20

August 1940

"Johnny, Hold that ladder still. It's wobbling. I've got to go up a bit higher."

As Johnny's hand tightened on the wooden ladder, he began to whimper.

"I can't hold it much longer. My arms ache. Ouch, and now I've got a splinter."

"Don't be a baby. I'm nearly up there now. There are a few I can't reach."

Suddenly Johnny's arms gave way and he had no choice but to let go of the ladder. Betty was left hanging on to a branch for dear life but found she could do so no longer. As she hit the ground with a bump, a cascade of purple damsons were scattered all over the grass.

The ladder had landed on top of Johnny and he let out a wail as a bump began to form on his forehead. Betty was beside him in a second.

"Shush, Johnny. Auntie Ellen will hear you."

But it was too late. Ellen was running down the garden to where the two children were, to see Betty cuddling Johnny who now had tears streaming down his face, creating channels in the dirt. He was looking very sorry for himself.

"My goodness! What *are* you two up to?"

She took Johnny into her arms to comfort him. He sobbed into her warm cardigan.

"We only wanted to buy you a birthday present, Auntie Ellen."

"A birthday present? What has that got to do with climbing the damson tree?"

Betty spoke up, giving her brother a look that would have curdled cream.

"It was to be a surprise. We were going to sell the damsons to the greengrocer and spend the money on your present."

Ellen smiled at these two precious children whom she had come to love as her own.

"That's a lovely thought, darling but you should have asked someone to help you. It's dangerous climbing trees."

"I know that now. Can we still do it though?"

"Yes, you can still do it, dear, but wait until tomorrow when Uncle William will be here and can help you. How do you know the greengrocer will buy them? Have you asked him?"

"Yes, he said he would. He is going to give us fourpence a pound."

"Fourpence? Well, that sounds a lot of money. You will be rich in no time."

"We don't want to be rich Auntie. We just want to buy you a present."

"Tell you what we'll do. We'll go along to the post office and open up a savings account for you. I'll start you off with a shilling to buy two stamps and then you stick them on a card until you have enough to spend."

"That sounds great. Thank you Auntie.

And so it began - the children's saving accounts got started and it set them on the right road from then on. They would do lots of little jobs to earn money from collecting eggs to cleaning shoes. These often had to be gone over again but no-one complained. It was good to see the children enjoying themselves.

On the morning of Ellen's birthday Betty and Johnny ceremoniously handed her a small present. Johnny was jumping up and down in his excitement. Inside was a box which held a beautiful butterfly broach of vivid blue colours. She knew it had cost a lot of money and when she confronted William later in the day, he explained, looking rather sheepish.

"Well, I did put a bit towards it."

"A bit? It must have cost a fortune."

"Well, okay, a bit more than a bit. Don't let on you know though. They were so thrilled to give it to you."

She kissed him on the cheek. "Thank you darling. It's lovely."

***

Every bone in Patricia's body ached. She had been working for twelve hours with hardly a break. There had been heavy bombing in the night and casualties were many. Men, women and children were being brought into the hospital and the wards were bursting at the seams.

The crying of the children was the hardest to cope with. Each nurse would do her best to comfort but there was only so much a body could do. Patricia worked alongside the friends she had made in the hospital. There was wonderful camaraderie between them all. One of them spoke to her now. It was the night sister. She was a strict sister but got the best out of all her nurses with the kindness she showed.

"Come on Nurse. You need a break. You've got to take care of yourself as well, you know. Get off to the home and report back in six hours. And try to get some food inside you."

"Oh, Sister. You don't know how wonderful those words sound."

"Good. Off with you then."

Patricia made her way through the debris left by the night's raids. Dust still hung heavily on the air and made Patricia cough as it clogged her throat. Rescue workers, covered with dust, were still working relentlessly moving bricks with the slim hope that more people would be found. The toll had been high.

When she turned the corner into her road she was relieved to see the nurses home still in one piece except for a few broken windows. She entered the front door and walked through the hallway in a trance. Once in the communal kitchen she toasted two slices of bread and opened a can of baked beans. She washed it down with a cup of strong sweet tea. It tasted like nectar. After that she climbed the stairs and tumbled into bed, aware of nothing else until her alarm clock woke her for her next shift.

Even though she had only slept for about four hours she felt remarkably refreshed. She had only removed her dress and had slept in her underwear so it took only a few minutes for her to get dressed again. A quick cup of tea and a piece of toast and Marmite and she was on her way back to the hospital.

She had been at St Thomas's for six months and, although the work had been hard, she had loved every minute of it. She was so pleased that she had become a nurse. Taking care of people had made her forget her own grief and she found she hardly ever thought about Alec now. Sometimes she could barely remember what he looked like. They had had so little time together. It all seemed like a far distant memory.

A few days later Matron called her into her office and bade her sit.

"I want to tell you, Nurse Linden, how pleased I am with your efforts here. You have been a great asset, but I am now going to give you the opportunity for a change. I have been asked to recommend nurses to serve in Suffolk and Norfolk where the airmen, both British and Canadian are based. They are getting a lot returning home injured and

nurses are badly needed there to care for them. I want to know if you are interested. I will be sorry to lose you, though we have another batch of trainees coming in next month so that will help. What do you think? You can have some time to think it over if you need it, though I will need to know by next week. You won't be going just yet. There are all the formalities to sort out first."

Patricia raised her eyebrows and opened her eyes wide.

"Well, I can't say it's not a surprise but I don't need to think about it. I would love to go. Not that I'm not happy here, but it would be a challenge. And something very different. Are any of the other nurses going?

"Yes, in fact you will have some familiar faces around you. Nurse Blake and Nurse Wilson have already said they want to go . And I have yet to ask Nurse Jenkins."

It was just twenty one days later when the four girls set off for pastures new. There was an air of excitement in the group and as they squeezed onto the packed train they didn't even mind not having any seats. They sat on their suitcases in the corridor and watched the countryside whizzing by. It seemed to take an eternity to reach their destination with all the hold-ups and when leaving the train had to struggle with all their luggage onto a bus to take them to the hospital.

As they took their seats the conductor came up to them with his ticket machine.

"Where to my beauties? Don't often have beauty queens on my bus."

The girls laughed and although they knew it was only banter it lifted their spirits no end.

"We're off to start nursing at the hospital. Is it far?"

"No, my duck, only about a mile. Be there in no time."

As they went to get their money from their pockets and offer it to him he shook his head.

"No, You put that away. It's my treat."

And with a broad smile and a wink he turned the handle producing four tickets which he handed to them. The journey passed quickly and in what seemed only a few minutes they were alighting from the bus. They left with good wishes from the other passengers ringing in their ears.

As they went through the gates to the hospital in the distance they could see planes coming and going and when in formation the noise was deafening. But there was something reassuring seeing the boys in blue strutting their stuff. Patricia felt a lump in her throat.

They had to report to Matron's office where they collected their uniforms of grey cotton with white collars and cuffs and the tiniest of little caps to pin on their heads. Patricia thought them very fetching but wondered how she was going to keep hers in place with her abundance of hair.

As they made their way to the nurses residence with their cases and bundles they felt quite excited. It was a long, low building with six rooms all housing four beds in each. They had been issued numbers and found themselves in pairs so did not feel too estranged from each other. Patricia was with Sandy, so named because of her hair colour. Her name was actually Gillian. The girls had become good friends and had been together for a while now so Patricia was pleased they were close. The other two, Amy and Clare, were in the next room.

There were three small bathrooms nearby and further along the corridor they found a kitchen. Although it was not large it was well equipped with all the basic things they would need to produce nourishing meals. They had handed their ration books in at the main office.

"I'm not sure when we have to start work but I suggest we get something to eat whilst we've got the chance. Let's see what there is in the cupboards." suggested Clare, who enjoyed her food.

They found bread and baked beans so hastily prepared them on toast with a welcome cup of tea.

As it turned out it was lucky Clare had suggested getting something quickly as an hour later there was an emergency and all four girls were called to duty. They had only just had time to unpack their clothes and cram them in the small wardrobes when the bell rang. They quickly donned their new uniforms and pinned their caps into place.

An ambulance had arrived at the hospital with two badly injured airmen. They were suffering from burns and the girls were thrust straight into their work without having time for any qualms.

After that ambulances seemed to be arriving at all hours. Seeing these broken boys made Patricia's heart ache. The war was not going well for the allies and there was not a family in England that was not affected in some way with sons, husbands and fathers in danger. How anyone was still able to have optimism Patricia just didn't know and yet nearly everyone she spoke to felt the same. In spite of everything there was a stubborn streak that refused to think of defeat.

The four friends slipped easily into a routine of working, eating and sleeping. They were so tired when they tumbled into bed at the end of the day they said no more than to wish each other goodnight.

21

July 1964

When Sally began to have morning sickness she guessed she was pregnant. They hadn't planned to have a family so soon but now she was thrilled. She told Joe as they lay in bed that night and he was as pleased as she. They were so thankful that they were not still living in the flat. That would have been hard. But here in this wonderful house they couldn't wish for anything more. It was a house that needed children to fill the rooms.

Donald was still coming to the house and would turn up on the doorstep on the slightest pretext. This time he told Sally that he had inadvertently left some papers in the office that he now needed. She did not believe him but couldn't for the life of him think why he should want to keep coming to the house. It must be obvious to him that they had settled there and had no intention of leaving. She accompanied him to the office and stood watching him as he looked through the desk. It was of dark wood with numerous drawers and he went through these one by one.

She felt very uneasy and in the way but was not going to leave him alone. The desk was one of the places that she had not sorted yet but was determined to do so as soon as she had chance. He left without finding anything and seemed particularly peeved as he went down the path. He didn't even say goodbye.

When he got back and let himself into his dingy flat, he immediately went to the kitchen cupboard and took out a half-filled bottle of whiskey. He didn't bother about a glass but lifted the bottle to his mouth and slurped greedily. He was desperate. Unless he could lay his hands on some money pretty soon he would be in deep trouble.

His gambling addiction which, up until now, he had always managed to feed from money from his grandmother was now getting out of hand. The old bitch had only left him a measly two hundred pounds and that had long gone. He hadn't realised just how much money he had lost over the years until it had dried up. Like most gamblers he had

always thought he was on a winning streak. Just how much he was pouring into it to win he had not counted. Only the winning registered in his mind. He thought he had kept on top of it.

Only now was it evident to him that the costs had been far greater than the rewards. He was in deep trouble - and to some very unsavoury characters. They would be ruthless in their efforts to recoup their money and would stop at nothing - even killing.

He knew that there was something of great value hidden in that house. If only he could find it. If the truth be told, he did not even know where to start looking or even what it was he was looking for. He had planned to rip the house apart if necessary to find it once the old lady was out of the way. But it had all gone wrong when he had been turned out and that young chit of a girl had appeared from nowhere. Who the hell was she? She didn't even seem to know herself just why she had inherited the house from his grandmother.

He wasn't even sure if he would be entitled to the house if anything should happen to her. It was worth thinking about though. Some accident could easily befall her. He supposed it depended on whether she had yet made a will and thought it very unlikely, being so young. It was not something she would have even thought of. But how to find out. Time was running short.

There was one way he could find out, of course. Andrew Underwood would know. If he could get into his records perhaps there was a chance.

He knew of someone who could help - who owed him a favour.

22

Christmas 1940

Patricia and the other nurses were doing their utmost to make it a good Christmas for the men. After their long days of working on the wards they used any spare time to create paper chains and garlands to hang around the day room and had even put a few in the wards with Matron's permission so that the ones who were too injured to get out of bed could still enjoy the colour of Christmas.

May Simmons, one of the nurses who was rather rotund, had dressed up as Father Christmas. Someone had even come up with a beard, albeit rather straggly. No-one cared and they all gave her a stupendous welcome when she came in, playing along and acting as children.

"Oh, look! Here's Father Christmas."

She delved into the pillow case she was carrying and started to hand out small gifts to the men, just little things like packet of five Woodbines or a Mars bar. Cigarettes and bars of chocolate were well appreciated.

The atmosphere was electric and the laughter did the men more good than all the tonics they were taking. The feelings that were created that day were to some like escaping back into their childhood and gave a brief sense of security. Patricia wondered if they should not celebrate Christmas more than once a year. There was so little to relieve the boredom of these valiant men. All of them, no matter what their injuries were itching to get back in the air.

The hospital received quite a few parcels donated by people in the local community and if the Canadians or Australians got things from home they willingly shared them with the English boys. There was a special camaraderie amongst the men. Each one was willing to give their life for another so a few things from home were easily parted with to give a bit of pleasure.

The patients who were more recovered were allowed a small amount of alcohol and Sally and the other nurses had got together with them to make an evening of it. An old piano had been donated by the local squire and now one of the Americans was sitting at it and hitting the keys, some a bit out of tune, so that the others could sing.

As Patricia sat laughing and chatting to a young pilot from Hastings she felt someone sit down beside her. She looked round and saw the handsome face of Gus, an airman from Vancouver, whom she had been caring for.

"Hi, Patricia. I am allowed to call you that now you're off duty aren't I?"

"Well, I'm not exactly off duty, but I guess it'll be alright."

Gus was serving in the Canadian Air Force and had been brought into the hospital with only a 50-50 chance of survival two months before Patricia had arrived there. When Patricia had first cared for him he had still been very frail but had made a remarkable recovery. He was almost unrecognisable now from the man she had first seen. He had crash landed and his face and body had been badly damaged. She had nursed him when his eyes had still been bandaged and had written letters home for him. Because of this she had got to know his family well through the ones he had received back and which she had read aloud for him. She had grown very close to him - much more than she should have done, she knew that. But, though it was not encouraged, it was very hard not to form relationships in this sort of cocooned environment. These boys were a long way from home, as were most of the nurses, and they craved something to replace the families they had left behind.

He was still having to walk with the aid of a stick and placing it up against the table sat down beside her. As he slipped an arm round her shoulder the English airman smiled and tactfully got up to go to join another group. Patricia was a very popular nurse with all the men and was very much admired and respected. She had helped many of them retain their sanity when the odds had been stacked against them. She understood it wasn't just their bodies that needed healing.

As the days passed and Gus got stronger she knew it wouldn't be long before he would be fit enough to report back for duty and she dreaded the day. She knew he felt the same. Not that he didn't want to get back to fighting the enemy but they would have to say goodbye. This wasn't a place he would return to. Not unless he was again badly injured and she didn't want that.

It troubled her and she had confided to Sandy about her feelings for him even though it was personal. There was not much the girls didn't know about each other. Many a secret was shared in the small hours of the morning when they would be on duty together and most of their patients were sleeping.

Gus was trying to persuade her to go to a hotel for a couple of

nights with him before he had to go back and she longed with all her being to agree. But she was still a married woman in the eyes of the law, though she truly believed Alec to be dead. Nothing had been heard of him.

Sandy agreed with Gus. She thought very highly of him and knew how fond he was of Patricia, and she of him if she wasn't mistaken.

"Look, you can't go on like this. You need a break and nothing has been heard of Alec. I really think you would have heard by now if he was still alive. I'm sorry, my dear, to be so blunt, but we can all see how much Gus loves you and you must grab at happiness whilst you can. We are surrounded by grief the whole time and if there is anything we can do to help ourselves we must."

Patricia looked at this dear friend who had been such a rock for her when she had needed one. She knew she spoke sense.

"OK, I promise I'll think about it."

"Well, don't wait too long. The way he's going on it won't be long before he's back with his unit."

Although Patricia was exhausted by the time she got into bed, she lay awake for a long time letting Sandy's words go over and over in her mind. She did love Gus and knew that if she did not go away with him and make the most of the precious time together she would regret it for the rest of her life. What if he should be killed - would she ever forgive herself?

She had made up her mind before she finally dropped off into a restless sleep.

23

1964

The two men had chosen a night when the weather was wet and very windy to cover any sounds they might make as the younger man broke into the building. The lock was easy for this accomplished thief. He had had far worse to deal with and it took only seconds before he was letting Donald into the hallway. He would keep watch whilst Donald attempted to find what he was looking for, though he wasn't sure what that actually was and he hadn't asked. It was none of his business.

As Donald's accomplice was standing in the shadow, doing his best to keep out of the driving rain Donald quietly closed the door and climbed the stairs. He knew which office was Andrew's and quickly let himself into the room. He had brought a torch with him and switching it on headed for one of the filings cabinets. If he had thought this to be a simple task he was unpleasantly surprised. He had surmised that everything would be in alphabetical order so proving easy to find the name of Bancroft or Westwood. He was wrong. The first file he looked at had letters from all over the alphabet. Everything was filed higgledy piggledy. There was no feasible reason for the order they were in. Perhaps they were in year order. But that was no help either.

He was sweating around the collar now, partly in fear of being caught but more in frustration. He had been searching for twenty minutes and found nothing of significance. When the voice came from his accomplice he nearly jumped out of his skin. His nerves were in tatters when his partner-in-crime called from downstairs. Someone was opening the front door and ascending the stairs. Donald panicked and as Andrew entered the room brought the torch down on his head. The old man fell to the floor before he had time to realise what was happening.

Donald didn't wait to see if the old man was still breathing. He just fled.

Andrew lay still as the blood ran onto the carpet creating a dark stain.

It was all over the town the next day when Sally went to the shops. Everyone was talking about how Mr Underwood had been attacked and now lay in hospital. He had lain on the floor of his office until his secretary had arrived for work the next morning for although he had regained consciousness he had been unable to get up because of dizziness due to loss of blood.

Sally didn't go home but went straight to the hospital. When told by the Ward Sister he was not allowed visitors she left some flowers with a message saying she would return in a couple of days.

When she did so she found him sitting up in bed, looking rather frail but in good spirits. On his head was a large bandage with a trace of blood on it.

He was pleased to see her and she gave him a hug.

"Have the police any idea who it was?"

"No, my dear. It's a complete mystery. It's not as though I keep any money on the premises. The files were apparently in disarray, so someone must have been searching for something." He gave a little chuckle. "They wouldn't know where to look with my filing system. It is unique and only my secretary knows how it works."

"Why were you there at that time of night?"

"Oh, I'd forgotten some papers which were needed for a meeting I was going to early the next morning and decided to pick them up. I won't do that again in a hurry. It's lucky we have a red carpet." he chuckled. "I understand there was quite a lot of blood"

Sally felt like hugging him. He was so dear to her.

"How long do you expect to be in here?"

"Oh, they're keeping me in another night and then hopefully I'll go home tomorrow."

"Well, let me know if there's anything I can do."

As Sally let herself into the house she felt uneasy. She hadn't mentioned to Mr Underwood that Donald had been to see her again. She thought he had enough on his plate.

She removed her jacket, opened herself a tin of soup and, once she'd eaten it, decided to go back into the office and see if she could shed any light on what the man actually wanted.

She became quite engrossed in her task and found herself wading through various bills and receipts, some dating back years. She found them fascinating, especially comparing prices with today. There were old bills for decorating the house for such small amounts it didn't seem possible.

It was when she came upon some old letters that she felt her excitement rise. Most of them were from the second world war. She had been born during the war but her mother had never spoken about it and Sally had always been intrigued especially when she had worked on a project at school. She remembered going home to her mother and asking questions as they had been told to do by the teachers but her mother had said she didn't have time to rake over the past. Her father had been a little more helpful and told her of his days in the Navy but she had learned very little. She gathered the letters together and seating herself in the leather chair opened the top envelope and started to read. The first letter she opened was from Patricia.

Dear Gran and Gramps

I am sorry I have not written sooner but it is so busy here I do not get much time to myself but please do not think I am not happy. I am enjoying every minute. I am so glad that I chose to be a nurse.

I have made some good friends, my closest one is Sandy. We get on so well together. It is like having a sister with me. We usually have the same shift if possible and although we are not encouraged to get too close to another person in case we are separated it is very hard not to.

We see some terrible cases from the bombing and it is hard to cope with the children's grief if they are left orphans or if their fathers are serving abroad and they have no-one but we must be strong as well as showing compassion and tenderness. It certainly makes us forget our own troubles.

I hope Johnny and Betty are well. When I see the injured children I feel so glad that they are safe with you in Hitchin. Do give them a big hug and kiss from me and tell them I miss them very much. Have they been falling out of any trees lately?

I miss you too, of course, both of you. Please take care.

Your affectionate granddaughter

Patricia. xxx

24

January 1941

A light covering of snow lay on the road as Gus manoeuvred the jeep along the narrow street. He and Patricia had driven to Norwich where a friend had recommended a small family guest house. It was just big enough to be comfortable and homely, they were told. And more importantly the owner was very discreet and accepting of the needs of her guests in these troubled times

As they carried their overnight bags into the lobby Patricia felt as though she was in dream. She had agreed, after much persuasion on his part and being encouraged by Sandy, to come away with Gus but was still haunted by feelings of guilt.

Mrs Lamb, the owner of the house, welcomed them as though they were old friends. She understood how hard it was for the serviceman and women in these troubled times. She had two sons serving in the Navy and knowing she could not be there for them when they needed her she would be there for other's sons in a similar plight. It was her way of helping and just hoped that if her boys were in a similar situation then some kind person would be helping them.

It was not, in fact, a hotel but just a house that with her boys away had a couple of spare rooms. She only let one at a time, just in case one came home on unexpected leave.

The room they were shown into was pristine clean and bright even on a dark January afternoon. It was clearly a young man's room with pictures on the walls of ships. Model ones stood on the shelf that had been erected along one wall.

"I've cleared the wardrobe for you so you will have somewhere to put your clothes."

"Oh, Mrs Lamb, you needn't have worried. We have very little with us."

"No trouble my dear. My boys don't have many clothes so I just

put them all in one room. Well, I'll just leave you to get settled in. If there is anything you want just give me a shout. The bathroom is just along the landing. You can't miss it."

The room was sparsely furnished with just a bed, wardrobe and small chest of drawers. There was not even a dressing table but had it been the Ritz they could not have been happier. Just to be away from the hospital for a while was heaven. The room overlooked the garden, that had once been Mr Lamb's pride and joy with his prize blooms but was now turned into a large vegetable patch to help the war effort. Only a few flowers remained and being the middle of winter were not yet brave enough to show their heads above the soil.

It was early afternoon and Gus suggested they go for a walk whilst the sun was still doing it's best to shine, for there were heavy snow clouds hanging in the distance and it looked as though they were due for another downfall. Patricia donned her warm coat, a thick scarf and her beret and they walked out of the hotel, her arm linked in his. He, like most Canadians, was looking extremely smart in his uniform and many a female head turned in his direction as they walked.

The smell of fish and chips assailed their nostrils as they turned into a narrow road with a row of shops on either side and Patricia suddenly realised how hungry she felt. She had only indulged in a hurried breakfast before packing her bag. Time was not something that was plentiful in their busy days. Patients had to come first.

The fish shop was busy and the queue stretched out of the door and along the pavement as this was the only food you could buy that was not on ration. As they joined the other people huddled together against the north wind Patricia found herself relaxing and starting to enjoy herself. Other people in the queue were soon chatting to each other and it only seemed a minute or two before they were at the front. Their fish and chips were placed onto a large sheet of newspaper and they added lashings of salt and vinegar. The smell was delicious.

As they strolled along the road eating, all the tension of the last few months seemed to flow from her body. Here she was with a man with whom she had fallen in love. She did not fool herself that it would last in these troubled times but that seemed only to intensify her happiness. Every moment was precious. She felt she had to grab any pleasure by the scruff of the neck and not let go.

By the time they got back to the hotel she had lost all her doubts and by the time they tumbled into bed she let all her pent-up passion flow. She let him undress her, hold her, kiss her and eventually enter her, enjoying every moment. He was a tender lover and withheld his passion

in order to bring her to satisfaction.

This was the first time of many. For two days they lost themselves in each other, completely uncaring of what the future may bring. They loved with such passion and afterwards when they were satisfied would lie in each other's arms and sleep.

When the time came to leave it was with great reluctance that they packed their bags and loaded them into the jeep. As they said their goodbyes to Mrs Lamb, Patricia felt she was saying it to an old friend, so kind had the dear lady been.

The journey back was a bit of a trial as there was a light blizzard blowing most of the way but when they eventually reached the hospital, there was no doubt in Patricia's mind that she had done the right thing and she was pleased that she had succumbed to Gus's offer of the nights away.

If only she could have been sure of their future. She knew he must soon return to his unit and in a way these two nights with him was only making it harder to face his going. She had enjoyed his body lying close to hers. She hadn't realised just how much she had missed the contact with another, especially in the early hours of the morning when he had slipped his arm around her and held her close.

25

France 1941

Alec lay hidden in the hayloft of the old farmhouse as voices drifted up to him from below. He tried to move his aching limbs without making a sound. He had been there for only three nights but to him it seemed like an eternity. He was waiting for the instruction to be ready for evacuation. He found the waiting was the worst thing. His body seemed to be tense the whole time. Although physically he was partly healed, mentally he was far from well. The nightmares would still come to him almost every night. During the day he found it difficult to remember the events of that dreadful day but at night in his sleep the pictures were vivid. He would wake, his body wreathed in sweat and he had to have the bed covers loose around him. If they were tight he thought he was suffocating beneath the bodies. Sam's face would be staring at him with unseeing eyes.

The old man who owned the farm and his frail wife had been like grandparents to him over the past weeks. They spoke only a few words of English that they had learned from the men they had helped and he certainly spoke no French so conversation was limited but it was amazing how they seemed to know his every need and would do their utmost to give it to him.

When he had first been brought to them he was completely unaware of the world around him. He lay unconscious for most of the time and the weight had dropped off him through lack of food. It was two days before he could manage to hold a drink and even longer before he was able to take any sustenance from anything solid. The old lady had made him broth from any vegetables she could find in their garden and mashing them to a pulp did her best to coax him to eat.

They knew that if they were caught harbouring an English soldier their lives would be taken from them without a qualm, but even with this knowledge they still did whatever they could to outwit the Germans. Alec was not the first they had helped and God willing there would be many more.

He lay now, trying to remember just what had happened to him. It was, even after all this time, very hazy in his mind.

When the troops had been forced to retreat from the German army, he along with all his comrades, had fled towards Dunkirk hoping to be picked up by one of the hundreds of little ships that had come to the aid of the trapped forces. Thousands had made it but many lay dying after they had received fatal wounds. He would have been one of these had he not been shielded by the body of his pal.

Sam and he had been friends from the first day they had met. They had clicked right from the start. Being the same age and both from Hertfordshire, they found they had a lot in common and completed their training together. Each would have given his life for the other. And this is what Sam had done. He had taken the full force of the shrapnel that had hit them and had died instantly. Alec was injured and being unconscious had lain beneath him. Luckily he was not visible to the German soldier who came across them and who would have put bullets into them both just to make sure they were dead. Sam got one in the head, although he had long gone to meet his Maker.

Alec had lain there for two whole days before he was discovered by a French farm worker who had heard him groan. He had been lifted onto a wagon and taken firstly to a hut in the woods then on to a nunnery where he was kept hidden and treated by the nuns who risked their lives to help others. If caught, they would be shown no mercy. This did not stop them from doing God's work. They were taught not to hate in their religion but the feelings they had for the Germans could not be described as anything else.

Perhaps it was as well that Alec lay only semi-conscious for many weeks as he healed. He was not to know what went on around him. It was only now that he had to make decisions and there was only one thing he wanted to do and that was to get back home. As his clothes had been covered in blood and removed when the nuns first started to care for him, no-one knew who he was so he was not officially reported to be alive.

He was now to be taken by resistance workers to eventually be picked up by the RAF and flown back home. This was not without risk as so much relied on the weather and allied forces being able to get through unseen by the enemy.

In the meantime there was interminable waiting to get through. His thoughts sometimes caught glimpses of the past when he and Patricia had been together. But he couldn't hold the images. It felt as though he was trying to grasp a bubble. Her face would drift through his mind like a wreath of smoke. He would catch a glimpse of her smile and for a second would feel the warmth of her touch. When that happened he wondered what she was doing now. Did she or anyone know he was alive?

26

1941

William had not mentioned Bernard though Ellen knew he must be thinking about him often. They had decided when Bernard had left the diamonds in their charge to create a hiding place for them. They thought about putting them in the bank but were not sure whether awkward questions would be asked as they were on personal terms with the manager.

So one evening when they had been on their own in the house they had gone up to the top floor where their was no linoleum and lifted a floor board. Beneath this was a cavity that William had made marked by a brass ring. They had carefully placed the velvet bag holding the diamonds into the space, replaced the wooden lid and put the floorboard back in place. Here they would stay until Bernard was able to return and claim them. They hoped and prayed that this would, one day, be possible.

Now, over three years later, they were still there. Neither William or Ellen ever spoke of them. She felt his loss for his friend. Rumours were rife of atrocities the Jews were suffering but, like everyone else, they were powerless to help.

When Patricia returned to the hospital after her three days with Gus she was told there had been an urgent telephone call from her mother and she was to call her back.

She experienced a feeling of apprehension as she asked the operator for the number. It wasn't like the family to contact her for no reason. The first thought was that something had happened to her grandmother so when it was she who actually answered the telephone she let out a breath of relief.

"Patricia, dear. We have some wonderful news for you. There has been a telegram from the War Office saying that Alec is alive."

There was silence on the line.

"Patricia? Are you there, dear?"

"Yes, Gran. I'm here. It's just such a shock. Where is he?"

"He's in a hospital in London. We don't know any more than that at the moment. I have the telephone number here for you to call them."

Patricia wrote the number down and as she replaced the receiver

Sandy appeared in the corridor. She saw how white Patricia was and immediately put her arm round her.

"What is it, love? Is it bad news?"

Patricia held back a sob as she answered.

"No, no it's not bad news. It's my husband. He's back in England. I don't know any details - just that he's alive."

She tried to avoid Gus for the rest of the day, but knew she must face him sometime. Her feelings were in a turmoil. She was happy and glad but, at the same time, sorry.

When she finally managed to get hold of the hospital where Alec was she spoke to the matron and was told that he was in a poor state and would only be allowed visitors for a short time.

When, at last she told Gus, he had been very understanding and said she must go to see her husband no matter what. It was as though they were just friends instead of the lovers they had been. Patricia's feelings were in a turmoil. How could she love two men at the same time?

The next few days were filled with new arrivals and it took some time to arrange a day's leave. She set off with mixed feelings. She had no idea what she would find. It was as though she was going to visit a stranger.

The journey seemed never-ending; the train was packed and stuffy and extremely slow, seeming to stop every half hour. Her nurse uniform helped her to get a seat, of which she was extremely grateful. She had been working twelve hour shifts over the past few days. By the time she finally got to the hospital it was late-afternoon. It was cold, dark and unwelcoming on the streets of London. The blackout was enforced and there were no lights to cheer the gloom. Rubble lay in all directions from the bombing and it took her a long time to reach her destination..

She was glad to enter the hospital. It, at least, was warm and inviting. Being a nurse, she felt a sense of security when she was in familiar surroundings. She had been told to go straight to the matron and as she was shown into her office she was near to fainting. She, who was normally a strong and resilient person who could handle most situations, felt as vulnerable as a child leaving its mother for the first time. It occurred to her that she had not eaten since her early breakfast.

Matron could see how bad she was and immediately called for a hot, strong cup of tea to be brought to her - with plenty of sugar in it.

Patricia gulped it as though she had not drunk for a week. It tasted wonderful. There were also three biscuits which matron insisted she eat.

When she had finished Matron took her hand.

"You must be prepared for a shock, my dear. Your husband has been through a great deal. He was badly injured in France and although was nursed out there, has wounds that have not healed as they should have done had he gone into hospital at the start. However he is responding to treatment now but it is not his body I am concerned with so much as his mind. That still has a long way to go. He is greatly affected by all that has happened and the horrors he faced. Apparently, as far as we can gather, it was his best friend who saved him by dying himself and shielding your husband with his body. Your husband is wracked with guilt and I'm afraid that is not helping his recovery. Now I'll get a nurse to show you where he is."

Patricia was led along to the ward. It was quite a small one with just six patients in it. Had she not been shown to where Alec lay she would not have known which one he was. She didn't recognise the man who lay in the bed. His once dark hair had turned almost white and his skin was as pale as snow.

She pulled a chair up to the bed and sat down. He didn't move. He lay as stone. She felt at a loss to know what to do. She, who could care for strangers with no qualms, now felt completely helpless sitting beside her own husband. There was nothing she could find to say so she just took his hand in hers. He jumped as though he had been punched in the face and as he opened his eyes they stared at her in horror. Then as his gaze held hers a smile reached his lips. Still she could not speak to this man, this stranger.

They sat like this for at least ten minutes and then his hand began to squeeze hers and she felt him come back to her. Then as quickly as she felt the pressure of his hand it disappeared again and he snatched it away.

It was an hour later when she finally left his bedside. She had been given another cup of tea and the offer of a sandwich which she had gratefully accepted, smiling at the nurse and thanking her. Although everything seemed calm and quiet Patricia knew what was going on behind the scenes and the façade. Didn't she face the same thing herself day after day. The nurses were trained to give a quiet air of confidence to their patients and visiting relatives even if they felt as unsure as everyone else.

As she walked away from the hospital she decided she would travel directly to Hitchin. She had the urge to see her mother and grandmother and just be held in their arms as a child again.

As she stepped through the front door of her old home it was like stepping into another world. Back into a wonderful past where everything had been cosy and warm.

Ellen and Susannah were delighted to see her and cosseted her as the child she wanted to be. They held her, fed her, talked gently to her and eventually tucked her up in her own bed with two stone hot water bottles. A fire was burning in the grate and as she lay snug in her bed she watched the reflection of the flames on the ceiling and felt she was in heaven. Tomorrow she would face the world again.

She left them the next morning feeling refreshed and with new hope.

27

1964

The police had drawn a complete blank as to why Andrew Underwood had been attacked. As far as he could see nothing had been taken but he was more vigilant in his comings and goings with regard to work and did not stay late in the evening for any reason whatsoever.

He had his own theory and couldn't help thinking that perhaps Donald Bancroft had been responsible. There was no-one else he could think of who would want to search his office.

Because of these uneasy feelings he decided to call on Sally to put to her that perhaps she should make a will. But how to do this without alarming her in any way he was not sure. So he decided to just turn up one day on the pretext that he was passing and had some time to kill before going to another appointment.

She welcomed him warmly and invited him in for a cup of coffee and as they sat she told him of the photographs, letters and journal she had found.

"If you have time I'll fetch them for you to see." she said and when he answered in the affirmative left the room.

As she handed him the items he smiled with pleasure and took them from her. He then proceeded to put the names to the faces in the photographs. As he had known the family for many years and had become a friend to them all he recognised many of them. He was even in one of the photographs himself as a much younger man.

Sally was fascinated by all the memories and feeling at ease with him decided to tell him of the experience with the mirror.

To her surprise he didn't laugh at her but looked at her with understanding in his eyes. He spoke quietly.

"That's strange, you know. Ellen always did say that mirror was haunted. During her last few months she swore she could see things in it that weren't really there. I just thought it was an old lady's ramblings. Not that she was the type to ramble. She was a very intelligent lady right up to the end."

"What sort of things did she see?"

"Oh, well, I didn't really take much notice, I have to confess.

Something about when the children had been younger. And once she told me she had seen William. I just thought it was wishful thinking."

As Andrew was about to leave he realised that he had not spoken of the very thing he'd come for - the will.

"I don't really like to bring this up, my dear, but have you considered making a will - now you have this property to consider?"

"Gosh, no. I hadn't. I thought wills were for old people."

"Oh, no. It is very important if you own something of value such as this house. I know some people feel superstitious about making one as they feel they are tempting fate - but everyone should. Call in the office sometime and I'll help you to arrange it. Bring your husband as well, of course. You see" he added "Donald could still inherit should anything untoward happen to you."

When she told Joe that evening he laughed

" Gosh, we're only young. We're not going to die yet."

"I know, darling, but if anything did happen to me then apparently Donald would get the house and you'd get nothing. That's how the old lady's will stands at the present."

"Well, it still seems a bit ghoulish to me, but I guess the old man knows what he's talking about."

So Joe and Sally went along to the office and duly made a will. Andrew felt a sense of relief. He had the feeling that Sally was now out of danger.

As it happened his feelings were not without substance. Andrew's secretary of many years had recently taken ill and had been replaced by a much younger woman and on hearing this Donald had immediately set about getting to know her, sensing this was the only way he was going to find out anything. He dare not risk breaking in again.

When he discovered that Sally had made a will he was furious. He had been making plans to be rid of her and knew there was no way now that he could obtain access to the house.

Sally looked closely at the cheval mirror and thought how neglected it looked. No matter how much she washed it the white paint still looked a murky grey and the gilding on it was almost non-existent in parts. When Joe came home that evening she brought the subject up.

"I've decided to paint the old mirror, Joe. The one in our bedroom. If you could help me carry it down the stairs I'll lay some newspaper on the floor in the kitchen and do it there. I've bought a small tin of white paint and a tiny tin of gold. I can't wait to start it."

Between them they carefully carried the mirror down two flights of stairs to the kitchen and whilst Joe worked in the garden Sally was in her element painting the old mirror and restoring it to its former beauty.

She had finished the first coat, allowed it to dry and was just about to start to top coat when there was a ring at the doorbell and Joe came down the stairs with Donald in tow. Sally looked askance and was just trying to think of an excuse to get rid of him when he suddenly went ghostly white and fled from the room uttering something about an appointment he had forgotten. They heard the front door slam as he made his exit.

They looked at each other in puzzlement.

"Well, what do you make of that?"

They did not notice the reflection in the mirror. It was Ellen Bancroft and she was smiling.

28

1941

It was intended for Alec to stay in the London hospital for a month but because of the bombing which caused him to wake screaming with terrible nightmares it was decided that he should go into the country. He was finally settled in a hospital that catered for shell-shocked victims in the Cambridgeshire countryside. Although the many planes could be heard going over there was only the occasional night raid and it was far safer than London. His nightmares were less frequent in the quieter surroundings. But he was far from well and on the rare occasions when Patricia was able to visit he still did not always recognise her. She would sit with him and hold his hand when he would let her.

Gus had gone back to his regiment in March and though they corresponded regularly their relationship had lessened considerably. When he had found out that Alec had returned he knew it was not fair to put any pressure on her and they had seen less of each other before he left.

It was just after he had walked out of her life that Patricia had confided to Sandy that she was pregnant with Gus's baby.

"Oh, my God, what are you going to do?"

"You tell me. I'm at my wit's end. I just can't tell my mother or grandmother. Not with Alec lying in hospital. I'm so ashamed."

"When's it due?"

"Well, it's easy to work that out. I only went away with him the once, so by my reckoning it must be due in October."

"Does he know? I mean did you tell him before he went away?"

"No, I couldn't do that to him. He had enough to worry about what with going back into war. I didn't want to load him with another burden. He has to keep a clear head. I am very fond of him, you know. If Alec had not come back I like to think that Gus and I could have been together after the war. Oh, that sounds awful doesn't it? I am so glad that Alec is safe and sound." she paused for a few seconds. "Well, he is safe but I don't know about sound. He hardly recognises me when I see him."

Sandy put her arms around Patricia and held her.

"I don't know what to say, love. You're sure in a pickle. Have you thought about trying to get rid of it?"

Her companion looked shocked.

"Oh, no. I couldn't possibly do that. I have to face this somehow. I just can't present Alec with a baby though. The only alternative I can think of is to have it adopted."

She spoke the next words on a sob. "That answer seems unbearable at the moment, but I can think of no other."

"Well you probably won't show for a long time so you'll have a chance to think about it. When are you next visiting Alec?"

"Next Tuesday. I'm taking a couple of days leave."

Back in Hitchin William and Ellen sat in the spring sunshine in a sheltered part of the garden. Johnny and Betsy were at school and everything was peaceful. The war that was raging in Europe was forgotten for a few moments in this lovely garden.

Both sat in silence breathing in the scents of the apple blossom that was already adorning the trees. Ellen loved this time of year.

But as they sat it was not long before the war again intruded on their thoughts. It could not be held at bay for long.

Ellen thoughts turned to her granddaughter and her unfortunate husband. Alec was showing only a little sign of recovery. It seemed the experiences he had suffered in France had made deep indentations in his mind that could not be healed. It was hoped that he would be able to return home for convalescence but each time the subject was raised there was a set-back.

If they had but known it Alec did not want to return home. He felt a deep sense of security in the hospital being cared for. When Patricia came to visit him he felt bewildered and confused.

On William's mind was his friend Bernard. He had heard nothing first hand from him but the rumours that reached England were devastating. The suffering the Jews were experiencing were now common knowledge. They could no longer be hidden, although the stories that got through were scant.

He still had Bernard's diamonds safely hidden away at the top of the house. He and Ellen had spoken of them only last evening each wondering what to do with them. They had spoken of them when they passed the lounge on their way to bed and were unaware of the person sitting hidden in the high backed leather chair. Donald's ears pricked up as he caught the odd word or two. There was just enough spoken to raise his interest.

Donald had escaped going into the forces due to a heart murmur that had been caused by him contracting rheumatic fever when he was young. It was not really enough to prevent him serving his country but he had played on it and then pretended to be devastated that he couldn't become a soldier. The one thing that was not a factor in his personality was a conscience. It was something he had not had as a child and still did not as a man.

What, he wondered, were his grandparents talking about. The word diamonds had been enough. He was annoyed that he couldn't hear what else they were saying as they mounted the stairs. He mounted the stairs immediately after they did in the hope that he would hear more but the doors in this old house were good solid ones and only muffled sounds came from within their bedroom.

He spent a lot of time at their house now, not having a good relationship with his father. If truth be told his father was ashamed of him. He thought him a coward. He saw through his son's ploy to keep out of the forces. Although Daniel would never admit it and probably didn't even see it the two men were very alike in character. They were both weak men who would always seek the easy way out whenever possible. Perhaps that was why they disliked each other so much for they saw their own faults reflected.

In the days that followed him over-hearing his grandparent's conversation he built up a determination to get to the bottom of it. It started as a tiny seed in his mind and grew to proportions he would never have envisaged. It would take over his life.

29

London 1941

As Mary Bolton took her baby from her breast and covered herself she gazed down at him and felt such love she felt she would burst. He was just two months old and starting to take note of his surroundings. She even got the odd smile or two. Though some said it was wind, she knew differently. They were definitely smiles.

He was clothed in a blue romper suit which Mary's mother had knitted for him. She had knitted about six in all - in every colour she could find. It didn't matter if he was a boy and sometimes had to wear pink There was a shortage of wool in the shops so she had meticulously unpicked old jumpers and carefully rewound the wool. She doted on her grandson and worried about his uncertain future with this terrible war going on.

Jack, his father, was serving in the Navy and at present was enjoying a few days embarkation leave before rejoining his ship.

Tomorrow was Mary's birthday and he was going to surprise her with a trip into the West End. There was little choice for anywhere to go but he had heard that The Windmill Theatre had a saying 'We never close' so that was where he was going to take her. Mary's mother had happily agreed to look after the baby.

The next afternoon he told Mary to put on her best togs because they were going somewhere special. At first she was reluctant. She had not left the baby at all since his birth and was apprehensive. But Jack would have none of it.

"It's your birthday, love, and we're going out. This is the last chance we'll have for a long time."

Mary looked at her husband, so handsome in his uniform, and knew she might not see him again for many months and so relented and agreed to leave her son. After all he would be in good hands.

With Mary dressed in her one and only decent suit of pale blue with a matching beret on her dark hair and Jack in his sailor uniform they made a handsome couple as they walked through the gate. Mary's mother watched them go with pride. And they looked back to see the baby in her arms.

The journey into town was a bit hair-raising. There was a lot of bomb damage and craters were evident in the roads. Traffic had to weave and wend to avoid them. Buses and trams were erratic - if there were any at all. Tram lines had been damaged and men were busy trying to repair them. It took them a long time to reach their destination but reach it they finally did and when they entered the theatre Mary's spirits lifted. It was packed and as they took their seats she looked round in wonderment. She had never been anywhere like this before and the excitement coursed through her.

The show was breathtaking. No-one would ever know there was a war on and it was forgotten completely in those few hours. Mary thought the costumes rather scant and in some cases non-existent, leaving nothing to the imagination. She knew her mother would be quite appalled even though she was broad-minded. But once the dancers had been on the stage going through their routines for a while all prudishness was forgotten - although they were not allowed to move in the nude and chose poses that flattered. The curtains discreetly opened and closed at the right time, just leaving enough time to glimpse a tantalizing sight of bare flesh. The show caused a few eyebrows to rise along with a cacophony of wolf-whistles.

During the performance sirens could be heard in the distance but everyone tried their hardest to ignore them. In the interval Jack bought drinks at the bar and as Mary was breastfeeding she chose a lemonade. She stood enthralled by all that was going on round them. Most of the men were in uniform and even some of the women but the rest, like Mary, had put on their glad rags and looked as colourful as possible to brighten up the gloom of war-torn London if only for a short time.

Mary was quite sorry when the performance ended and the audience started to trickle out of the theatre. Everyone walked slowly as if they were reluctant to enter the real world again. They had escaped to paradise for a while.

The journey home was even more traumatic as it was dark; the roads and pavements filled with hidden dangers, the slabs having been pushed up at awkward angles by bomb damage and even lamp posts presented difficulties as pedestrians could not see them and were forever walking into them. Cars lights, and even hand held torches, had to be shielded by covers so as not to attract the enemy in the skies.

They managed to get on a bus for part of the way and then had to walk the rest. Mary was glad she had worn her comfortable shoes. Even so her feet were beginning to hurt. But she felt good. They laughed together as they clung to each other. She was glad she had agreed to come.

That was until they neared the road where they lived. They heard the commotion from a way off and then when turning the corner froze to the spot. The street was unrecognizable. Two houses had received a direct hit and three doors away had been Mary's. It was no longer there; just a pile of smouldering rubble. She tried to run into the ruins and had to be held back by a fireman. A piercing scream was coming from her open mouth and Jack had to cling onto her. Although she was much smaller than him it took all his strength to hold her. Then she slumped as blackness overcame her.

When Mary came to, she was in her husband's arms and as he held her she looked up into his tear-stained face. She tried to rise to her feet but found her legs had turned to jelly. They clung together sobbing.

The next few days were the worst Mary had ever experienced in her life. The bodies of her mother and baby son were recovered from the rubble. She had known how much her mother hated going to the shelter so her father had assembled a Morrison shelter in the front room. It was an unsightly construction and her mother covered it with a cloth when it wasn't in use. In fact it resembled a table when covered. They had known it would not protect them from a direct hit but would provide them with safety if a bomb was dropped some way away. On this night it had been too close and they hadn't stood a chance.

Mary's father had been on fire-watch and although her mother had often said how much danger he was in, it was ironic that this had saved his life for had he been at home he would have died alongside her mother.

Jack was immediately given compassionate leave and he and Mary travelled to Bury St Edmonds where her Aunt Dora lived. On receiving the phone call she had offered to take them in without hesitation. It was not a large house but beds were shifted around to fit them in. They didn't have much to take. They only had the clothes they wore. Everything else had gone.

Dora did her best to comfort Mary but it was as if she had put a wall around herself. Her grief was so intense that she was in a dark cloud. Losing both her mother and baby she felt as though the sun would never shine again. She cut herself off from the world and retreated into a hell of her own making. She didn't want to smile again. It was hard enough to make herself swallow any food that was put in front of her. It was made even more difficult for her to cope because her breast milk was still flowing. She wished she had stayed at home and died as well.

Jack had had to return to his ship and Dora was at her wit's end. Mary had always been a favourite of hers and she just didn't know what she could do to help her.

She wrote to Sandy at the hospital and told her the tragic news.

At the end of a long shift Patricia found Sandy sitting on her bed in tears and immediately went to her pulling her into her arms. "Whatever is the matter?"

Sandy gulped and stumbled over the words. "My auntie has been killed in London."

"Oh, I'm so sorry. Were you close to her?"

"Yes, but that's not the worst of it. She was looking after my cousin's baby and he was killed too. He was only two months old."

Patricia's heart did a summersault. "Oh, how dreadful."

"Mum has got Mary staying with her at present and just doesn't know how to cope. She can't get Mary out of her depression. She won't even talk."

"Where is her husband?"

"He's had to go back to his ship. They only allowed him two weeks compassionate leave. Oh, I suppose you can understand why. There are so many people being killed. They can't give them leave indefinitely. If every soldier and sailor got leave when they lost some-one there wouldn't be enough left to fight."

"No, I guess not. Are you going to apply for leave?"

"I think I'll have to. I can't leave Mum to cope on her own. Not that there will be much I can do. But I can give her some support. My cousin and I were once very close. We grew up together. I may be able to get through to her. I hadn't even seen the baby, but I know how thrilled she was when she had him. Oh, poor Mary. This bloody war. When will it end?"

At that moment Patricia felt her baby move for the first time.

30

Alec showed little sign of improvement and as beds were so badly needed it was decided by the doctors that he be moved to a convalescent home to recover. There was no more the doctors could do for him and they were urgently needed for other patients. He still reacted badly to any loud noise and could not even cope with the sounds of the air raid sirens let alone any bombs being dropped.

He was moved to a country house that had been opened up to soldiers in the small town of Woburn in Bedfordshire. It had first been in use during World War 1 and was still a peaceful haven for men who needed it.

On the day Alec was moved Patricia had arranged to be with him and settle him in. She was to travel with him in the ambulance.

The day was much worse than she had envisaged. She had arrived at the hospital in good time to help get him settled in the ambulance but it was quite an ordeal. He was still very withdrawn and only spoke the odd word or two and although Patricia did her best to bring him out of himself it was a one way conversation. It was so hard now to relate him to the man he had once been and he still seemed like a stranger.

She was now six months pregnant but had put on very little weight, due to her busy working life. She rarely had a chance to relax at the home where the nurses resided. Even when she had a chance to sleep there were so many comings and goings that noises would reverberate continually. Reluctantly, some of the nurses resorted to sleeping tablets but Patricia had resisted the temptation due to her pregnancy. She was afraid of harming the baby.

The journey to the hospital seemed to go on for an eternity and it was late afternoon when they arrived. After a quick snack Patricia helped Alec to bed and settled him for the night, promising that she would visit as soon as she was able. She wondered if he had even heard her. It was as if he was in a little world of his own into which he had retreated.

The journey back to Norfolk was a nightmare. There was one hold-up after another and it took several hours. On the latter part she managed to hitch a lift with a pilot whom she had met in a café and she realised how she had missed conversation. Just to talk with a man who wasn't injured or in pain but full of life. Most of her patients had to be mothered and now, for the first time in months, she was on equal footing with another human being,

Sitting on the train had given her time to think and try to find a solution to her problem. She had avoided going home to her mother and grandmother, having the excuse that she was under a lot of pressure at work.

What was she going to do? She knew in her heart that she was going to have the baby adopted. There was no other way. But she had come to love this tiny being growing inside her and the thought of parting with it tore her in two. Never to see it again once she had given it away seemed something that was impossible to contemplate.

She thought of Mary, Sandy's cousin, and the grief she was suffering and a tiny thought entered her head. At first she thrust it aside but by the time she had got back to the hospital it had grown. She knew what she must do.

When she put it to Sandy it was met with surprise and rejection but then as Patricia spoke to her Sandy began to see the logic of it and it didn't seem quite so unfeasible.

"Look, Sandy, I know I have got to part with this baby. No way can I take it home. I can't tell you how much I want to keep it. I cry every night before I go to sleep. But if I have got to give it away I would rather it be to someone I can trust. I know I've never met Mary, but what you've told me of her makes me think she is a lovely person."

"Oh, she is, but there is so much to consider."

Patricia broke in on her words.

"What, Sandy? What is there to consider? She has lost her baby and I've got one going spare, so to speak. What better solution can there be?"

"Well, when you put it like that....I guess you're right."

"I know I'm right. Can you arrange for me to meet her and talk to her about it? Trouble is, I can't ask for much more time off. I've had so much lately. Perhaps I could meet her halfway somewhere. That way I wouldn't need to be away from the hospital for too long."

"I'll write to her. How much do you want me to tell her?"

"Perhaps it would be better if you wrote to your mother and she could put it to her in a gentle way. She must still be feeling very vulnerable. And of course her husband would have to agree."

"Oh, I'm sure he would be delighted. He would do anything for her."

***

So the two women met at the small hotel where Sandy's mother, Sophie, had arranged for her and Mary to stay for a night. She hadn't wanted Mary to have to travel on her own.

When Patricia arrived at the hotel Sophie and Mary had already checked into their room and were waiting in the coffee lounge for her. Patricia recognised Sophie at once - she was an older replica of Sandy. She stood and held out her hand.

"It's nice to meet you, Patricia. My daughter has told me a lot about you. It sounds as though you get on really well."

"Yes, Sandy and I have a lot in common."

She turned to the girl still seated and her heart went out to her. She looked so small and vulnerable. Her eyes looked as though she had not stopped crying for weeks. She wore a simple cotton dress in pale green with white collar and cuffs. Patricia thought the colour did little to enhance her complexion. Then she immediately felt contrite. Obviously this poor girl had lost all her belongings in the bombing and had been given someone else's cast-offs. She didn't know whether to be formal and offer her hand or to give her a hug. She decided on the latter but the girl only responded coolly.

The words that came from her mouth seemed stilted and inadequate but she could think of nothing else to say so just said "Hello Mary. It's nice to meet you."

Sophie could sense their embarrassment so butted in and offered for Patricia to join them for a light lunch and on her acceptance they went through to the dining room and chose a table near the window, though little could be seen out of it as it was criss-crossed with tape in case of bomb-blast damage.

A waitress came to take their order and they all chose a ham salad, though when it arrived they needed a magnifying glass to find the ham. Still, that was war and it was accepted.

The pudding more than made up for it though. It was a bread and butter one and although it was made with dried milk it was delicious.

Talk came with difficulty and it was a while before the main reason for them getting together was broached.

It was Sophie who brought it up.

"We're very indebted to you for thinking of Mary when considering adoption, my dear. It must be so hard for you."

Patricia had promised herself she would not cry but found it impossible not hard not to let the tears fill her eyes and run down her cheeks. She quickly dabbed them away with a handkerchief.

"Yes, it's is - very hard and I really don't know at this stage just how I am going to cope when the time comes. But I know it must, and as I said to Sandy, if I have to give my baby away I would rather it be to someone I know and trust. Oh, I know I don't really know you yet Mary, but I have heard a lot about you from Sandy and knowing it will help to ease your pain will help me in some way."

Mary spoke for the first time. "Thank you, I promise I will look after your baby as if it were my own. But I do realise that it never will be. You will always be its mother."

It was these words that helped Patricia dispel the doubt in her mind. Even if she knew in her heart that they were not true they drew her to Mary and she would trust her with her unborn child.

On parting Patricia gave Mary another hug and this time the other girl responded and clung on to her for several seconds.

They agreed to correspond through Sandy and Patricia promised to keep Mary up to date on how the baby was faring.

On the journey back she felt as though a weight had been lifted from her shoulders. She owed it to Alec to protect him from the truth of what she had done.

31

October 1941

Patricia worked at the hospital until two weeks before the baby was due. Any other time this would not have been possible but nurses were needed so much during these times that an extra pair of hands was not to be refused and, even though she was put on light duties and menial tasks, she was pleased to be working.

When the time came for her to leave the hospital and travel to Bury St Edmunds she and Sandy hugged and held back their tears. Both knew that for Patricia the coming weeks would probably be the hardest she would ever have to face.

It was arranged for her to stay nearby to Mary with a friend who had been told of the circumstances. She was to have a home-birth and a midwife was called and told of Patricia's decision along with the arrangements for the adoption. She accepted it without question. Who was she to judge? She was a kindly soul who had been a midwife for many years. She knew what pain Patricia was going to feel.

It was a strange time for Patricia. She seemed to be in limbo, partly wishing the time away but also dreading the time when she must say goodbye to her baby.

Her family was still completely unaware of her condition. She had not visited home for a long time. She longed to see her mother and grandmother but could not bring her shame on them. It was easy to deceive, saying how busy they were at the hospital that she was unable to get leave. She kept in touch by post and any letters that came were passed on by Sandy. They were not to know that she was no longer there.

It was a crisp October day when her baby came into the world. She had a short and easy labour and it was only five hours until she was holding her baby in her arms. It was a beautiful girl, weighing in at seven pounds. Her dark hair lay tight against her head and when she opened her eyes they were of the deepest blue, the colour of sapphires.

The love she felt when she held this tiny person to her breast was like an ache. She was going to breast-feed her for a couple of weeks to give her a good start. She knew it would make it harder to part with her, but in these times of shortages and lack of food she wanted to know that she had done her best for her daughter.

These two weeks were the happiest but saddest of her life. She hardly slept because she didn't want to waste the precious time spent with her baby and would lie and look at her for hours so as to imprint the image of her on her mind forever.

The last night she didn't sleep at all. She didn't want the morning to come and she knew if she slept it would come all the quicker.

She rose at nine and dressed her baby girl for the last time. She had spent her money on a beautiful white nightdress with roses embroidered on the yoke. It had been made by an elderly lady who lived in the village whose hands were twisted with age but could still create a thing of beauty.

When the knock came on the front door Patricia froze. She heard her landlady walk to open it, and then voices. She knew the moment had come that she must say goodbye to the most precious person in her life.

Her tears flowed down her cheeks, dampening the baby's dark hair and the lovely nightdress.

As she handed her to Mary she spoke in hushed tones.

"Could I ask one favour?"

"Anything." Mary answered.

"If you haven't already decided on a name, would you call her Sally? Ever since I was a little girl I've wanted a daughter call Sally."

"I think it's a lovely name."

"Thank you."

The two women hugged with the baby between them. Their's would be a tie that would never be broken.

On the day she said goodbye to her daughter Patricia received a letter from her mother that Sandy had forwarded to say that Alec was coming home at last. He would be home in two weeks time.

As Patricia sat on the train and watched the countryside fly by she resolved that she would devote all her time to helping Alec recover.

32

September 1964

There were still a lot of boxes for Sally to go through and one by one she would bring them downstairs and tip the contents onto the dining room table. She had decided to put all the photographs in piles to throw away the ones of no interest. So many of the people she did not know and thought she would have no way of finding out.

Perhaps she could invite Andrew Underwood to lunch one day. He seemed to be the only person who could help. Her mother was going to be visiting in a couple of weeks so perhaps that would be a good time to ask him.

She telephoned him and his secretary said he had someone with him at present but she was sure he would call her back as soon as possible.

It wasn't long before the telephone rang and she heard his voice.

"Why hello, Sally. What can I do for you?"

"Well, though it is partly what you can do for me, I thought it would be nice if you could join my mother and me for lunch one day on the 28th or 29th. Which ever day suits you."

"Let me have a look in my diary." she heard him rustle the pages. "29th would suit me better. I'm free all afternoon on that day."

So it was arranged for him to come for twelve thirty. Sally hoped it would be a nice day so they could have lunch in the garden.

It turned out to be perfect; one of those Indian Summer days when the sun shone and still had warmth in it. She and her mother carried a small garden table from the shed and dusted it down. The chairs were garlanded with cobwebs but once they had been brushed and the table covered with a pale green cloth it looked most inviting.

Sally thought her mother seemed a little distracted but was too busy preparing lunch to say anything. She had made a chicken casserole and prepared a side salad. For pudding she had made crème caramel She had even bought a bottle of sparkling wine. This was the first time she had actually entertained since moving to the house, except for her mother, of course, but she didn't really think of that as entertaining. She found she was enjoying herself immensely.

Andrew arrived on time and Sally showed him down the stairs and into the garden. He accepted a glass of wine with pleasure. Her mother offered to dish up the lunch but Sally insisted she sit and talk with Andrew, so she left them to it. She went back into the house and got the hot plates out of the oven along with the casserole.

Andrew could sense Mary's unease and knew he must put her mind at rest.

"Don't worry, my dear. Your secret is quite safe with me. I won't say anything to Sally that would upset you. I could tell when we first met that you were worried."

Mary managed a smile and let out a sigh of relief.

"I know you wouldn't say anything. It's just that perhaps I feel guilty. I should have told her years ago. It never seemed to be quite the right time. One minute she was too young and the next too old. I don't know what other people do in the same situation. I just dread the day when she finds out. What if she blames me for keeping it from her all these years. She remembers coming here, you know. I've tried to brush it off and told her she imagined it. But I feel the longer she is here the more the memories come back. After all, we spent two nights here and it was such a lovely visit."

There was no time to say more before Sally came through the back door carrying a tray.

"Could you just bring the casserole through for me, Mum?"

"Of course dear. Anything else?"

"Oh yes, I've forgotten the salt and pepper."

The meal was delicious and Sally felt immensely proud of her efforts. Even the crème caramel was perfect.

They sat and talked of inconsequential matters for over an hour whilst they were eating and when they had cleared the table and carried the dirty crocks indoors to be put in soak and washed up later, they went up to the dining room where the table was covered in photographs.

"My, my, you have got a lot here, my dear." Andrew exclaimed.

"Yes, well, I don't like to throw them away until I know they are not important. Of course I know they are not actually important to me but I feel responsible in a way. Ellen Bancroft did entrust me with her house and I like to think she would approve of me doing this."

Andrew and Mary exchanged a quick glance which was missed by Sally as she had started to pick up a small pile of photos.

"I'm sure she would, my dear." Andrew patted her hand.

As they turned the photographs over in their hands and looked into the faces Mary suddenly tensed as she caught sight of Patricia smiling up at her. She was immediately transported back in time to that day when she had been given the most precious gift of her life. As she turned to

Sally she almost caught her breath. The likeness was so uncanny. The clothes and hairstyle may be completely different but the faces were so alike. She quickly managed to cover the photograph with another of the garden.

"This is interesting. You can make out the trees that are here now and see them as they were years ago. And look at that tiny rose bush. It's the one that is now clambering over the wall."

"I'd like you to write on the backs of any photographs where you recognise someone, please Mr Underwood. Then I can go through them another time."

Andrew had never enjoyed himself so much. He sat for two hours with Sally and her mother sustained by numerous cups of tea relishing in the memories that the photographs evoked. Some were discarded but most he was able to put names to.

He was still there when Joe got home from work and was invited to stay for dinner but he declined, not wishing to outstay his welcome. He promised to get the photos that he was taking away to study back to Sally as soon as possible.

33

November 1941

Alec improved in leaps and bounds once he was ensconced back in the old house. They had been given the back bedroom at the top of the house overlooking the garden and the peace and quiet enveloped him. He was even sleeping better and was very rarely woken by a nightmare. He and Patricia grew close again and it not only helped him but her also. Of course, not a day went by that she did not think of her baby but she could look at the memories in a more detached way. It was as though it had happened to someone else and she was looking on.

She hoped she would get pregnant again but it didn't seem to be happening. How ironic, she thought. When she hadn't been trying she had fallen straight away.

When Alec was better she took a job at North Herts Hospital in the town. Nurses were still desperately needed. She was glad to get back to doing something useful. She was a good nurse and in no time at all had been made up to Sister, carrying a very responsible job.

She wrote regularly to Sandy and received letters in return which she avidly read. There was always the odd reference to her 'cousin's baby girl' without giving anything away, so Patricia knew Sally was thriving and healthy. There was even a photo sent on occasion which Patricia would look at when on her own. She would kiss the lovely face that gazed back at her. She wanted to show her grandmother but didn't know how to do so without giving anything away so she put on a brave face.

Her undoing was when Sandy came to stay.

Alec had gone back to visit his old regiment and have a medical to assess whether he should return permanently. He would be gone for three days so the girls would have a chance to talk.

Patricia couldn't wait for Sandy's arrival and walked to the station to meet the train. As she walked along Walsworth Road a convoy of tanks went by accompanied by other military vehicles. She was enveloped in a deluge of wolf whistles and she waved to the soldiers as they passed.

The platform was busy as usual with lots of men and women in uniform, some with their kit-bags on the ground beside them.

The train pulled into the station belching a cloud of steam and when at last it cleared Patricia caught sight of her dear friend. She was wearing her nurses uniform as was usual when travelling. If you were dressed as a nurse or in uniform you usually got preferential treatment, though it did not always guarantee a seat. Many an hour could be spent standing in the corridor. And then, of course, you were lucky if it was a corridor train. If it was at least there was a toilet to use.

The two made their way through the throng and hugged when coming into contact. Both spoke at the same time and their voices mirrored the same words. "Oh, it's so lovely to see you."

They laughed together and arms round each other's waists made their way from the station and out onto Walsworth Road. They were so busy talking they seemed to be home before they knew it.

After introducing Sandy to her grandmother, Patricia showed Sandy to the small bedroom on the first floor at the front of the house. It was cosily decorated in pale blue as it was the bedroom that Johnny normally slept in. He had gladly given it up for a couple of nights and agreed to sleep on a sofa in his sister's bedroom.

Johnny was now a well contented child and no longer needed his sister's protection but still loved being with her. When they had first arrived it had been them against the world and they had formed a closeness that would see them through their lives even when apart.

He still played the little trumpet and was actually getting to be quite good at it. He had built up a collection of tunes which he could play and often gave impromptu concerts. Betty, having a good voice, would accompany him and many an evening was passed by the family enjoying their performances.

Sandy changed out of her uniform into a light floral skirt and pale blue blouse. She, like Patricia, had very little opportunity to wear anything feminine and it was a real treat. She ran the brush through her hair and then ran down to join Sally in the garden. It was a perfect Spring day and the garden was awash with colour as the girls strolled around it. Sandy was enthralled with the place. Over the back wall of the garden was an apple orchard just coming into blossom. Sandy's eye caught the rope swing and she immediately let go of Patricia's arm and hitched herself onto the wooden seat..

"Oh, this is wonderful. I've always wanted a swing. You are so lucky."

"Do you know I haven't been on it for years? I was hardly ever off it when I was little. Here, I'll give you a push. You can go really high on it and see all the gardens."

Late afternoon the girls prepared a picnic to have on the lawn. They made dainty sandwiches of Marmite and cucumber and some of raspberry jam. They couldn't have enjoyed them more if they had been at the Ritz. The grass was a little damp so they sat on the old wooden bench. and as they ate Patricia broached the subject that had been prominent on both their minds - her daughter. She had made sure her grandmother was not in earshot.

"How is she, Sandy?"

"I heard from Mary two days ago. She knew I was seeing you so she sent me something she thought you would like. I've got it in my suitcase. I hope it's not too painful for you"

When, later she placed the tiny wrapped parcel in Patricia's hands it was opened with such tenderness it could have been a butterfly. There lay the beautiful embroidered nightdress that Sally had last seen on that dreadful day six months ago.

She could not stop the torrent of tears. It was as though a dam had burst. Sandy held her and let her cry, not uttering a word. There was nothing she could say.

34

1964

Andrew Underwood has become a regular visitor to the house and Sally had grown very fond of the old man. She had never known her own grandfathers and had always envied friends with one. So in a way he had become a surrogate one.

He had got on well with her mother when he had been to lunch and that pleased Sally. He had talked of his dear wife and the loss he had felt when left on his own. His son had come over from Canada for the funeral but had returned soon after because of business pressures. He had tried to persuade his father to return with him to live but the old man had said it was too late for him to start a new life at his age. And, although he was way past retiring age, he loved his work and many of his clients had become his friends, such as Ellen Bancroft had been.

Sally had given him a new lease of life and he called on her whenever he got the chance. At first he had felt he needed an excuse but as time had gone on he knew he was welcome at any time.

He had made a few visits to go through the many photographs and letters with Sally. When he came across the one from Bernard dated May 1939 he handed it to her.

"Have you seen this?"

She took it from him and read the beautiful scripted handwriting.

"Dear William

It is with much sadness that I have to tell you of the death of my dear wife. She was taken by force from our home in the early hours of the morning along with my daughter whilst I was away on business three months ago and I have only just managed to find out what happened to them. I will not go into details as it is too raw for me to speak of. All I can tell you is that my heart is broken. I have been trying to leave Berlin to come to England but fear now that it will not be possible. We are very restricted in our movements and watched at all times. I feel it is only a matter of time before I too am incarcerated.

I will post this letter immediately and I hope it reaches you. I have my doubts. If it does and you are now reading it please accept my love and friendship.

Take good care of the small items I left in your care and remember what I told you at the time. If I do not return to reclaim them they are yours.

Goodbye, my dear friend. I hope we meet again.

Bernard."

As Sally folded the letter, she had tears in her eyes. Although she had never known this man she felt for him as though it were her own father. How terrible to lose your whole family

"I wonder if they ever did meet again. And what it was he left with William. Have you any idea?"

Andrew half closed his eyes and was thoughtful, trying to recapture a distant memory. He too had tears glistening in his eyes.

"There was something that William once told me but I can't recollect just what it was. It was so long ago. I did feel it was something of great value. But what happened to it I really do not know. I don't recall ever meeting Bernard. He was a good friend of William from their university days But I didn't really know him very well then. He was just the son of a client.

She put the letter back in it's envelope and laid it with the rest of them. It had put them in a melancholy mood and Sally changed the subject.

"I've got something to show you."

She took Andrew up to the bedroom where the mirror stood in pride of place.

"What do you think of my painting? It was painstakingly slow, but I enjoyed doing it so much. I' m not sure about the actual mirror glass. It is very spotted with age but I am reluctant to replace it. It somehow wouldn't be the same with new glass"

"Oh, I agree with you dear. You mustn't change the glass. It just wouldn't be the same. It looks beautiful. You have done a grand job. Ellen would have been very pleased."

As he turned away he caught a glimpse of a figure in a pale green dress who smiled at him. Sally noticed how pale he went as the blood left his face.

"Are you alright? You have gone quite pale."

He smiled at her. "I know what you mean now, my dear. I truly believe I have just seen your ghost."

35

1941

When Patricia had returned from the railway station after seeing Sandy board her train she went to her bedroom and taking the nightdress from its wrapping she clutched it to her. She sat on the bed and just held it. The tears came quickly again and she could not hold them back. This was how her grandmother found her. She hadn't knocked, thinking the room was empty, but had just walked in to lay some clean clothes on the bed.

Patricia's head was bent over the tiny garment pressed to her chest and when she looked up at Ellen it was too late to hide the tears. They were streaming down her face. Ellen looked at her granddaughter in dismay, her eyes widening.

"Oh, my dear. Whatever is the matter?"

Patricia couldn't speak. The sobs were choking her as she was taken into the comforting arms.

When at last she had calmed down and wiped her cheeks with a handkerchief, held out to her, she began to talk.

It all came out. Her brief affair, the wonderful weekend she had spent, with Gus, the consequences and the subterfuge that had been necessary to carry out to protect her husband from any more pain. She spoke of her beautiful baby, the precious tiny being she had had to give away.

When eventually she had finished talking the pain Ellen was feeling was almost akin to her granddaughter's. She had never felt so helpless. There was nothing she could do to ease the heartache. All she could do was hold her.

Even if she had known earlier there would still have been nothing she could have done. She knew that. Patricia had made the right choice - the one and only choice. No way could she have put Alec through the knowledge that she had been unfaithful whilst he had been lying injured in France.

She could not condemn. She knew how much Patricia loved Alec but she also knew what difficult times they were living in and how everyone needed a bit of comfort from whatever source could be found. But Patricia had paid a heavy price for the comfort she had found with Gus.

She just held her dear granddaughter and let her cry. She would have given her life for this girl. Now all she could do was offer her comfort.

When Alec returned home the next day it was with the news that he would be returning to his unit and resuming his soldiering duties. There was no doubt he would be sent abroad again and though he relished the idea to 'get his own back on the bastards for taking his best mate' as he put it, Patricia couldn't but help the feeling of *déjà vu.* She had to be strong for his sake and managed to hide her feelings well and put on a brave face but below the surface there was such panic she felt she would choke on it.

He left three days later and she threw herself into her work at the hospital, working every hour God gave her.

Ellen Bancroft watched her work herself into the ground and could do nothing. She often thought of her great granddaughter and yearned to see her.

Alec managed to get seven days leave before he, again, said goodbye. He did not know where he was going to be sent. Not France this time but much further away. He was going to join his comrades in Burma. This time he was not to make it home.

36

May 1945

It was with mixed feelings that a victory party was being organised. The war against Japan was still not won but with the German surrender in Europe a big sigh of relief was heard all over England.

Betty and Johnny were still with the family and had now grown into happy, well adjusted children. In fact, Betty was getting to be quite a young lady. Ellen had been a strong influence in her life and had taught her good fashion sense and all the niceties that went with good manners. They knew, though, that the time would come soon for them to return to London and to their mother. This the children dreaded. They had barely seen her in the last five years and only vaguely knew her. Their father, who had lost a leg through his injuries had never visited them. Most evacuees had returned to their families long ago but Betty and Johnny had been so happy with her that Ellen was reluctant to part with them. She would miss them dreadfully. She hoped they would return for visits, but knew this would be very unlikely.

Today they were going to enjoy the celebrations. Any long tables or trestles that could come to hand were being placed in various roads all over the town and no matter that they all varied in height, once they were laden with every manner of food available it was barely noticeable. It was surprising just how much food had been accumulated. Goodness knows where it had all appeared from.

The women and older children had made sandwiches, cakes, jellies and blancmanges of every colour imaginable and the younger children sat wearing home-made hats cut from old newspapers and painted. They were of all shapes and sizes, some so large that eyes kept disappearing beneath them. This mattered little as the faces visible were wreathed in smiles as they tucked in to the feast.

Someone produced a piano accordion and they sang and danced to the music of Roll Out the Barrel and Knees Up Mother Brown. The Lambeth Walk was the most popular and rows of men, women and children strutted up and down the roads. It was as though a large black cloud had been lifted and the sun shone through.

Johnny was very pleased when someone suggested he played his trumpet for them all. He blew with all his might, his cheeks round with the effort. He was given a standing ovation when he finished. Ellen felt so proud she thought she would burst.

The children were each given a 'victory' mug to keep and Johnny cradled his to protect it when they at last returned to the house. He was to have it for many years. Two weeks later it was wrapped and packed in his suitcase as they said their goodbyes amid hugs, kisses and tears. Their mother had come to collect them and stayed overnight. It was quite a gathering that walked to the station to see them onto the train.

When Ellen returned from the station to the empty house she sat down and wept. The silence was tangible. She had grown accustomed to having the children around and could not bear the thought of life without them.

Her thoughts turned to her great granddaughter. She would be four years old now. Patricia had still received the odd photograph of her through Sandy. There was one Ellen particularly liked of her with a big bow in her hair. The likeness to Patricia was outstanding and Ellen's heart ached to see her.

It was in September that Patricia received the letter that was to change her life. Sandy had given Gus Patricia's address with her permission and Gus had wasted no time in writing to her. Except for the time when she had met him in the hospital, he had come through the war unscathed and was now back in Canada. He would be coming over to England to, as he said, tie up some loose ends and wanted to see her.

Although Patricia could barely remember him after all this time she still felt her heart give a little leap. After all he was the father of their daughter.

"Would you mind if I invited Gus to stay whilst he's in England, Gran ?"

Ellen did not hesitate to answer.

"Of course I wouldn't mind. I would love to meet him."

After all, Alec had been gone a long time now and there was nothing more she would love than to see her granddaughter happy.

Gus was expected to arrive on Tuesday so when the bell rang on Sunday afternoon and a good-looking man in Canadian uniform stood on the door step, William, who had answered the ring, looked quite taken aback.

And when the Canadian spoke in a deep cultured voice asking for Patricia he was even more flummoxed. He hadn't been told of this visit.

Luckily Patricia had heard the doorbell and come to investigate. When she saw him looking so handsome and well, she too was speechless. When she had last seen him he was still not quite recovered from his injuries but, now that he had put on weight, he looked the picture of health.

The years rolled away in an instant and Patricia's heart did a somersault. Much to the surprise of her grandfather she let Gus take her into his arms and hold her.

When, six weeks later, Patricia told her family that Gus had asked her to marry him and she would be joining him In Canada, they were not surprised. They had seen the change in her over the last weeks and knew, as she, that time together was so important in this post-war era. So much had been lost. Almost every person who had survived had a hungry appetite to savour any happiness that came their way.

The couple were married at the Registry Office and a small party was held for them before they left for their new life in Vancouver. It was with mixed feelings that Patricia said her goodbyes. She was both excited and sad. Her grandmother held her tight, not wanting to let her go.

37

London Autumn 1945

Johnny sat on the rubble of the old bomb site and put his trumpet to his lips. As the sounds emerged he went into his dream world - back to Hitchin and his Auntie Ellen. He missed her so much.

When the children had arrived home to a new life with their mother and father things had started off badly and then got even worse. Their mother pretended to want them back but they were like strangers to her, so long had they been away. No matter how hard she tried to get close to them it was as if a barrier had been erected between them that was insurmountable.

With their father it was even worse. As he struggled around on his one leg he was bitter and angry most of the time. He still suffered from a lot of pain as he had tried various artificial legs. But each one became intolerable and he gave up before he had given himself a chance to get adjusted. Apart from the pain it was the frustration that really got to him. He had been unable to go back to his old job and had to do anything he could find within his limits. He went from one job to another never settling in long enough to learn anything. With the children he had no patience whatsoever and snapped at them for the smallest thing they did wrong.

When they had arrived back in London the children could not believe how it had all changed. Johnny remembered nothing at all about the area they lived in but Betty had expected to see the places she had known. But they were no longer there. So many buildings had disappeared and those that were still there looked out of place amongst all the bomb damage.

The children had been shown to their old rooms and couldn't believe how small they were. After their bedrooms at Hitchin these seemed tiny. They unpacked their clothes and squeezed them into the wardrobes. Betty found it hardest as she had quite a lot of dresses that Ellen had made for her from cast-offs. She had taught Betty to unpick and re-use the material to create new garments and Betty had become quite good at needlework. Of course she would not have the use of the sewing machine now but she was still good at hand sewing and didn't doubt she would manage.

She was now fourteen and didn't have to return to school. but managed to get a job helping a dressmaker who taught her the basics of tailoring. One day a week she attended a college and even went to evening classes to improve her skills. She was very happy and got a lot closer to her mother.

With Johnny it was different. He seemed to have nothing in

common with his father. And when he proudly got his trumpet out to show him and put it to his lips he was met with “Stop that bloody row. I can’t hear myself think.”

So Johnny had taken it to the nearest bomb-site and played - and played. He put his heart and soul into it and though the old trumpet had seen better days and had the dents to prove it, it still gave off a good sound when Johnny blew.

It was on a damp and windy day when he sat with his eyes closed and created the sounds that were to change his life.

On opening his eyes he was surprised to see he was not alone. A man stood some feet away, listening. He was leaning on a walking stick although he was not old. He had obviously been injured in the war.

“That sounds great, kid. Where did you learn to play?”

“Where I was evacuated - in Hitchin. Auntie Ellen gave me the trumpet when I was little and a teacher at the school helped me. Did you really think it was good?”

“I sure did. My mates and I are getting a little band together and we could do with a trumpet player. Do you think your Mum and Dad would let you come along sometime and have a go?”

Johnny could hardly contain his excitement. “Yeah, I’m sure they would. My dad hates me playing in the house. Thinks it sounds awful.”

“Well, how about I come home with you now and have a word with them. I’m Jess, by the way” He held out his hand to Johnny who shook it feeling very grown-up.

Jess introduced himself to Johnny’s mother and father and explained how he came upon Johnny playing and how impressed he was.

His mother agreed that he could go along to the band if she could go with him to make sure they were alright and above board . When she met the others she was quite happy for Johnny to join them a couple of times a week so long as it did not interfere with his school work.

There were three of them in the band besides Jess - Bob, Harry and George. They were all ex-servicemen who had met up at the club they had joined on being demobbed. They made Johnny very welcome and immediately recognised his talent on the trumpet. It was not long before he was playing with them at small gatherings such as birthday parties and weddings.

It was after one of these that Jess handed him a box and when opening it he saw a shining trumpet. Though not new, as it had been bought from the second-hand shop, it was in much better condition than his own one. He put it to his lips and found it hard to thank them because of the tears that were choking him. His old trumpet still held pride of place though and occasionally he would bring it out and lovingly play it.

The band went from strength to strength and became quite well known in the East End.

When they got a mention in the local newspaper he sent Ellen a cutting and she felt such pride. The cutting was the first of many.

36

Summer 1946

When Jack finally left the navy he returned home to get to know his daughter. Sally was a pretty child with dark wavy hair that had a slight auburn tint to it. She had a ready smile for anyone who spoke to her and was Mary's pride and joy.

She knew now, when she looked back on that dreadful time of losing her baby, that Sally had saved her sanity. Just to have someone to care for and nurture had given her a reason for living. It had brought her out of the blackness that had engulfed her that terrible night.

At first she wished it had been a baby boy but eventually came to realise that had it been he could never have replaced her own son.

Jack thought Sally enchanting and from day one she wound him round her little finger. She only had to smile at him and he was completely enraptured by her.

Up until now Mary had lived with her aunt but it was a tight squeeze with Jack home so they decided it was time to find their own place. But though they searched high and low no place could be found. It wasn't easy with so many being made homeless because of the bombing.

It was getting quite difficult with the lack of space and Mary was starting to feel that nothing was going right when Jack received a letter from a naval mate saying he had invested his savings in a public house in Stratford and asking him if he would like to work for him. He couldn't believe his luck. The bonus was a flat above, which they could have. It didn't take Jack long to agree and thank his mate profusely..

The flat needed a lot of work to make it habitable as the pub had suffered some minor bomb damage but whenever he wasn't working in the bar Jack set to and between them he and Mary created a cosy home. They cleaned it up and bought a few tins of cheap paint which was liberally applied. Some fabric from the market was used to create curtains and cushion covers and Mary was very proud when her aunt paid them a visit and she was able to show her their lovely home.

In the evenings Mary helped out in the bar when Sally was asleep. She would nip upstairs and check on her every half hour.

The day Sandy forwarded her the letter from Ellen Bancroft her heart flipped over but when she opened the envelope and read the contents she sighed with relief. She read how Patricia had married Gus and gone to Canada with him. Although Sally had been legally adopted there had always been this dread that Patricia would want her back, even though it was not possible. And now she knew her child's real mother had gone away she felt at last that she was really hers.

Then the last paragraph caught her eye.

I would so dearly love to meet Sally. I have seen photographs and heard a lot about her. Could you find it in your heart to bring her to Hitchin so I could see her. I promise I will not compromise you in any way and would keep the reason for the visit a secret. I will leave it with you. You will be most welcome to stay at the house overnight to avoid a return journey in one day. Please write and let me know.

Yours affectionately

Ellen Bancroft

39

Sally could hardly keep still on her seat as the train drew into Hitchin station. It was the first time she had been on a train and the journey had been very exciting for her. Even simple things like seeing cows in the fields had given her a thrill. Her mother had made them some sandwiches to eat on the train and they had a little picnic. A rather large lady sitting opposite had kept them all amused with her tales of the blitz. She had a strong cockney accent and much of her speech was interspersed with cockney slang. Laughter had rang out in the carriage and the journey passed very quickly. Some were sorry it was over.

"Cor blimey we're 'ere already. 'Itchin it says on that sign. Next stop Scratchin." Sally had giggled out loud.

As the train pulled to a halt Mary gathered up the remains of their picnic and thrust them into the paper carrier bag. She then pulled on the strap to let down the window and leaned out to opened the door . Stepping down she put out her arms to Sally and lifted her down. It was rather a big step for little legs.

As Mary walked along Walsworth Road Sally was skipping along beside her. She was so excited. It was the best day of her life.

Mary looked at the numbers on the gates and front doors until she came to the right one and turned in the gateway.

"Now, you be a good girl, won't you?"

When they got to the front door it opened before they had a chance to ring the bell.

Ellen had been watching out of the window and now stood on the thresh-hold. Opening the door wide she bade them enter.

"Do come in. It's so nice of you to come. I hope the journey hasn't been too long for you. Did it go smoothly?"

"Yes, it was wonderful, thank you."

Sally looked at this lovely lady who was wearing the most beautiful blue dress she had ever seen. It was the colour of the sky on a sunny day.

Mary ushered Sally into the house, carrying the small bag with their overnight things in on her arm.

As soon as they had been shown the room in which they were to sleep Sally asked if she could go into the garden. She had climbed on a chair to look out of the window and seen the chickens scrabbling about in the flower beds.

She was enthralled and whilst the two women talked she ran around the tiny paths and chased the chickens. Her magic moment was when she came across three eggs which lay under the big plum tree. When she carefully carried them to her mother, Ellen said she would boil them one each for their tea.

Mary, who had had her reservations about making the visit in the first place now had the feeling that she had known Ellen for years instead of a couple of hours. Their was a strong likeness to Patricia which she could not really define. The hair colouring was different but the eyes that looked back at her were so like the ones she had looked into on that memorable day six years ago.

Ellen Bancroft had reciprocated the feelings that Mary had. She was so pleased that she had arranged this meeting. She now felt that her great granddaughter was in very safe and loving hands. She could see the bond between the two. It shone like a beacon. Mary's voice was never raised to the child; t was always loving and caring.

It was around four o'clock when Ellen had a visitor and Andrew Underwood joined them for a cup of tea. It was an impromptu call and although Andrew had said he would not intrude Ellen made him welcome as she always did. She introduced Mary as a friend of Patricia's from her nursing days and they chatted about inconsequential matters. It wasn't until two months later that Ellen told him who Mary really was and that Sally was her great granddaughter. She had made an appointment to see him to make provisions for Sally in her will. It was not a large amount but just enough to give her some security should she need it.

When the time came for them to part Ellen took Mary into her arms and held her.

"Thank you for coming, my dear. You have no idea just how much it has meant to me. You make a wonderful mother and I am glad that Sally is in your care. Will you ever tell her about Patricia?"

"Perhaps one day when the time is right. Though it will be very hard."

"Yes, my dear. I can guess it will be. I know I am being selfish but I would like her to know about Patricia. I hope she has another child one day, but who can tell? At least she is with Sally's father. I think that is some consolation. I am not sure whether she has ever told him about Sally though."

As the countryside flew by on the journey home, Mary sat and reflected on the visit. She was glad she had decided to go and meet Ellen. It seemed to close a door that had been standing open and now she felt safe in the knowledge that Sally was really hers.

Ellen sat quietly when Mary had left. Uncannily she also felt that a chapter had closed She had met a very important person and she would be able to write to Patricia and tell her how happy Sally was.

Although Ellen would never see her again, she knew that she would keep in touch with Mary and would do her bit to help in a roundabout way. There was always a nice gift in the post on Sally's birthday in the form of a cheque 'just to buy her some little thing'

40

Sally was in the basement kitchen preparing dinner when she heard Joe coming through the front door. She would not normally have heard him but this time he was making a lot of noise. Something landed with a clatter on the floor of the hallway. She came running up the stairs to see what was going on. She could not believe her eyes. At Joe's feet was a small crate with wire mesh and in it were two chickens squawking and flapping their wings as much as they were able in the confined space.

"Whatever are those doing here?"

Joe grinned from ear to ear. "Mac gave them to me. He is moving and couldn't take them with him. So, I said we'd have them. Just think, love, we'll be able to have our own eggs."

Sally screwed up her nose. "Pooh, they stink."

"That's only because they've been shut up in there all afternoon. I had to leave them outside in the yard until I came home. I'll let the poor things out in the garden. They're terrified at the moment."

He picked up the crate and struggled with it down to the side door leading to the garden. Sally followed him, shaking her head. They had never mentioned chickens before, though she had to agree it would be nice to have their own eggs.

It wasn't until a few days later when she was looking for eggs in the long grass that a memory came to her - of a day long ago when she had come across three eggs and carried them into her mother. She distinctly remembered there had been three. But how could that have been. Her mother had told her she had never been here before.

The memory wouldn't leave her and she was determined to phone her mother as soon as she was able. Mary went very quiet when Sally disclosed her thoughts and tried to fob her off again saying it was her imagination. Only this time Sally knew there was something wrong. Things just didn't tie up.

There had been other incidences that she had pushed from her mind. Just tiny things that had brought memories back such as the smell of a flower or the sound of a bird in the garden. She felt uneasy and couldn't settle. She was determined to get to the bottom of this when her mother next visited.

But something was to happen in the meantime that made her even more mystified.

There was a ring at the doorbell a week later and when she opened the door it was to see a man with a shock of blonde hair tumbling over his eyes. When he saw her he gasped.

"Auntie Patricia? No, it can't be. You would be a lot older if you were her. But you are so like her. I can't get over it"

Sally could see he was bewildered and felt sorry for him. Opening the door wider she asked him in, though afterwards she chided herself on her actions. She didn't know him from Adam. He could be anyone. But for some unknown reason she warmed to him immediately.

As he entered the hallway he looked around him with such pleasure shining in his eyes. It was as though he had come home. Sally couldn't help but catch his mood and she smiled.

"I guess you've been here before."

"Oh, it's just the same. And it must be eighteen years or more since I was here. I lived here, you see - during the war. I was evacuated with my sister, Betty. Oh, I can't tell you how much I've wanted to come back. We were so happy here."

Now Sally remembered where she had seen him before. It was in an old photograph. Even though he was much older he still had the same expression and the same blonde unruly hair. He had been holding a trumpet to his lips.

The next hour passed in memories being told. Sally had hurriedly prepared a snack for them both and she had sat and listened as he told her how he had come to live with Auntie Ellen and how she had given him the trumpet that had changed his life.

"We're playing at the Town Hall for a couple of nights and then at the Hermitage Hall for one. I was so thrilled when I was told and just had to come and see the old place."

"Where are you staying?"

"At The Sun Hotel in Bucklersbury."

Without thinking twice about it Sally asked him if he would like to stay with her and Joe and the smile that lit up his face was a picture to behold.

"Oh, I would love to. Do you think I could sleep in my old room. It's the small one at the front."

"Of course you can. I'll make the bed up for you."

"And I will give you two tickets so you and your husband can come along and hear us."

Which they did, and never had Sally been so moved as when Johnny had put that trumpet to his lips and played 'Oh, Mien Papa.' It brought tears to her eyes. Oh, Ellen Bancroft would have been so proud of her little boy.

Before he left he took one more wander around the house going into each room as though he was on a pilgrimage.

“Would you mind if I brought Betty back one day to see the old house again. She so loved it here.“

“That would be great. I’d love meet her. And thanks again for the tickets. We so enjoyed it”

“That was the least I could do. Thanks again for letting me stay.”

It wasn’t until long after he left that Sally remembered his words about Patricia and the likeness. She went to the box of photographs and found the one of Patricia. This was the person she had been sure she had seen before. She held the photograph in her hand and studied it. Then the realization hit her like a thunderbolt. Now she knew where she had seen this face before. It was in the mirror. It was her own reflection.

41

Autumn 1946

It was a warm, sunny day in October and Ellen was in the garden clearing some old foliage and putting it into a pile for William to burn on the bonfire when he got home. He was at the office and up to his eyes in work. They had lost several of their men during the war and even though they had taken on new ones who had been demobbed from the forces it needed a lot of patience and understanding to train them. Many of them had never been in the printing industry before and everything was new to them. So William had had to put in a lot of extra hours to compensate.

Donald had been coerced into the business but William found him lazy and un-cooperative. He never put himself out and only did the bare essentials that were asked of him.

It was in the garden that Ellen really enjoyed herself. She missed Patricia far more than she had ever expected to and although she had worked away for a lot of the last three years and they had not seen each other, now she was in Canada it seemed to Ellen like the end of the earth. She often thought about Sally and on several occasions had nearly picked up the telephone to ask Mary if they could visit again but knew that this would be unfair and unsettling for the child.

When the doorbell rang it broke through her thoughts and she quickly wiped her hands on her apron and went in to answer it.

As she opened the door she stepped back in horror. The man on the doorstep resembled a skeleton. Large, dark eyes stared back at her from a face on which the skin was almost transparent. He looked as though he would fall at any moment and Ellen immediately helped him through the door. As she told William afterwards she had not given it a second thought although she had no idea who he was. It had been obvious that he could do her no harm in his poor state.

It wasn't until she had him settled in an armchair and given him a cup of tea that she began to realise who he was. It was Bernard, William's German friend. When he finished his tea in silence he put his head in his hands and wept. Ellen felt helpless and did not know what to do so she let her motherly instincts take over and held him until his tears had all been spent.

By the time William had arrived home she had him tucked up in

Johnny's little bedroom. She still thought of it as Johnny's room even though he had been gone a long time. She still harboured a hope that one day he would come back.

Bernard was fast asleep when Ellen explained what had taken place. As she told her husband, their visitor had barely spoken a dozen words since he had arrived on the door-step. William said he would wait until Bernard awoke of his own accord before seeing him. He looked in on him several times during the night but there was no movement. For the first time in years Bernard slept as peaceful as a baby. For the first time in years there was no nightmare to wake him. For the first time in years he felt safe.

In the days that followed William and Ellen came to learn of the horrors he had been through. They had to coax the words from him at first and it took some time for him to be able to speak of the last few years. But when he eventually did it was as though a damn had burst and he couldn't stop. As he spoke they recoiled in horror.

"When I got back to Berlin, after I'd seen you, I found my wife, two sons and daughter had all been taken away. I tried to find out where but I could not. It was only many months afterwards that I discovered they had been taken to a concentration camp. I never saw them again. Did you receive my letter? I was not sure if it would reach you."

"Yes I got it so I know partly what you went through." William was reluctant to ask but felt he must. "How did you survive? How come they let you live?"

"I lived, my friend, because of my knowledge of diamonds. They needed me to cut and recreate stolen items." He spoke with bitterness in his voice. "Anything of value that they could steal from my fellow men. I was often tempted to tell them what I thought of them and refuse to help, and sometimes my temper got the better of me but little good it did. I was punished in ways I cannot tell you. So in the end they just broke my spirit and I did as I was told. But at least I am here now to tell the tale. I had nowhere to go so I thought of you and knew that I had to come and see you. I will not trouble you any further. I will catch a train to London to see what I can do for the other survivors. The ones that are left. There are not many of us and we are spread far and wide"

"You will do no such thing, Bernard. You will stay here with us as long as you wish. We have plenty of room and you will be most welcome. We will try to restore your health with Ellen's cooking."

Bernard put his face in his hands and sobbed like a child. William put his arms around him and held him. He could not believe that this was his robust friend who had been through the days of university with him. Who had run with him, played rugby and cricket, had laughed and talked into the early hours of the morning. So much fun they had had. He was now like an old man.

As Ellen settled him in the little bedroom and placed a warm stone bottle in his bed her heart went out to him. He had been through so much. They could only imagine what horrors he had seen.

She and William did their best to restore his health. They gave him every comfort and all the nourishing food he could take. He eventually got well enough to take short walks, but he was a broken man and it was only five weeks later when he passed away. He had no wish to live. William sat with him through his last hours. A minute before his friend took his last breath he smiled and looked right past William's head as though he had caught sight of someone. William turned expecting to see that Ellen had entered the room, but there was no-one there. As he turned back he saw Bernard still smiling. Then he took his hand as he closed his eyes and slipped away.

42

Sally was on tenterhooks. She couldn't concentrate on anything for thinking of her mother's visit and couldn't wait for her to arrive. She had to find out the truth. The photograph lay in her hand. It had hardly left her sight since Sally had taken a long look at it. When she had shown Joe he was as intrigued as she. Like her, he could not mistake the likeness.

Mary was travelling down by train and as Sally met her at the station they hugged. Her mother was looking extremely elegant in a coat of soft blue wool with a small fur collar. On her head she wore a matching hat.

Sally took her small suitcase from her and they walked to the house talking of mundane things. It wasn't until they were seated in the lounge with a cup of tea that Sally broached the subject. She passed her mother the photograph without speaking and watched as the colour left Mary's face and tears filled her eyes.

For a few moments she was unable to speak. Then she took Sally's hand in hers and in a voice so soft that Sally had to strain to hear it she said "You know then."

Sally opened her eyes wide.

"No, I don't know. That is the problem. Everything is a mystery to me. *Who* is this person and *why* do I look so like her?"

For a few moments that seemed to go on forever the person opposite her sat in stunned silence. The ticking of the old clock filled the room. Tears suddenly filled her mother's eyes as she answered.

"She is your mother."

Sally gasped and put her hand to her mouth. She then stood up and turned towards the window and after a few moments that seemed to go on for ever she returned her gaze to Mary.

"But, she can't be. You are my mother. I don't want another one."

Mary stood and gathered Sally into her arms.

"Sit down, my dear. It's time I told you everything and I hope when I've finished you won't think too badly of me." her voice became choked "I love you very much and couldn't stand losing you."

So they sat together on the sofa whilst Mary poured out her heart to her dear daughter and it wasn't until she had finished that Sally found she couldn't speak for her heart was so full of love for this person whom she had spent her life with.

To hear what she had been through and how she had lost her beloved baby in the blitz wrenched at Sally's heart. Tears were streaming down her face as her mother finished her story. She took her in her arms and rocked her as if she were the mother and Mary the child. And together they cried.

When, at last, they had both calmed down Sally forced herself to speak.

"Is Patricia still alive? And if so where is she? Not that I have any wish to see her. You are my mother as far as I am concerned."

"You have no idea how much it helps me to hear you say that. I have been so afraid all these years that if I told you I would lose you. I have no idea if she is still alive. The only person who may know is Andrew Underwood. We could ask him if you want to ."

"Of course, now it all makes sense. He said he held confidences that he could not tell me. He has known all along, hasn't he? He knew why Ellen Bancroft left me the house. She was my - my great grandmother. So, did we visit when I was a little girl? So I wasn't imagining it all. I knew I had been here before. When Joe brought the chickens home and I searched for eggs it brought such happy feelings to me. I love this house, Mum. Now I know why. It is because Ellen's spirit is here. I feel her when I am alone."

"Yes, she loved you very much, although she only saw you the once. She so wanted to do something for you and I would only accept the smallest help. I was afraid she would have pride of place in your life if you found out. Now I feel bad about it. She was a lovely lady and for her to leave you this house just goes to prove that."

"We'll get in touch with Andrew and see what he can tell us about Patricia."

43

1946

William and Ellen were completely unaware that Donald was lurking behind doors trying to catch words of their conversations. He was so sure that they had something of value that had belonged to Bernard. He had caught the odd word here and there which had led him to believe that Bernard had left something in their care and now it seemed it belonged to them and Donald being the ever greedy money-grabbing character that he was, was determined to get something out of it.

It sounded from what he had heard that whatever Bernard had left was still in the house. But where? Although they had often talked of acquiring a safe nothing had ever come of it. If it was money Bernard had left then surely it would have been put in the bank. No, he was sure it was hidden somewhere and he was determined to find out where.

The funeral had been a sombre affair with only William and Ellen in attendance. They did not know of any family Bernard had still alive so William had purchased a small plot in Hitchin Cemetery and laid him to rest with a plain but tasteful stone.

It said simply "*Bernard Goldstein, 1878 - 1946. dear husband of Rachel. Together again.*"

The small hoard of diamonds lay un-touched in the hiding place beneath the floor boards at the top of the house and here they would remain for many years but Donald never forgot that there was something to find. He was sure he would lay his hands on it one day. He would bide his time.

He knew that one day he would inherit the house. There were no other grandchildren to whom it would go. He would just have to patiently wait until his grandparents died.

But how long would that be? He was living a miserable existence in his opinion. Had he the intelligence to think about it, he would have appreciated how well off he actually was. He had everything he needed to make his life comfortable with no effort on his part. But when he looked around him and saw anyone with more his greed overwhelmed him. He thought it his right to the best that money could buy. He just did not have the money. But one day he would.

44

Andrew Underwood wasn't sure why Sally had invited him to lunch. He just assumed it was out of courtesy as her mother was visiting. But as soon as he entered the house he sensed something was wrong.

Lunch was eaten with the usual pleasantries and the topic of conversation was of mundane things but Andrew still had a sense of unease. It wasn't until they sat in the lounge over coffee that the real reason for them asking him became apparent. Sally told him of her discovery.

He felt uneasy as he sat with her and her mother. He knew that he must disclose confidences that had been entrusted to him many years ago.

He sat and related the story as he had known it and, although Mary already knew her side, for the first time she discovered what lay behind Patricia's decision to give up her baby. She wondered now why she hadn't asked more at the time but looking back realised that she had been so wrapped up in her own grief that she had not looked beyond it. Now she felt the anguish that Patricia must have gone through.

"I am sorry, Mary, that this has caused you pain, but I must say that I am so relieved that Sally now knows the reason why Ellen left her the house. I know Donald expected to inherit and there were times when I thought he would do so. He got very close to his grandmother over the last few years but I always sensed there was something behind it. I have never known him to be the caring person he was making out to be. In fact, I must confess that I was extremely worried over the circumstances of Ellen's death. I even let my suspicions be known to the police but there was nothing to incriminate him. The doctor said she died of a heart attack and there was nothing to show otherwise. Then when I read the letter she had left with me asking for Donald to be removed from the house I knew, more than ever, that there was more to it than we'll ever know. I just wish I had spoken to her more before she died. Perhaps it would have shed some light on it all."

"Do you know where Patricia is now?"

"Yes, she is in Vancouver and happily married to your father. They never had any more children. Ellen used to keep me up to date and let me know all about them. They did fly over for the funeral, but were unable to stay for long. They didn't even hear the will read and I think she just assumed Donald would inherit. They are quite well off and don't need the money."

"Did she mention me?" Sally tentatively asked.

"Not to me, she didn't, but then I don't suppose she thought I would know anything about you. I have her address if either of you wish to contact her."

Sally looked at her mother and saw the pain on her face. Mary answered.

"Perhaps one day we will write. After all, she is about to become a grandmother."

Andrew's eyes lit up. "Oh, congratulations. I am so pleased for you. It will make the house complete to have a child in it again."

"Maybe, after the baby's born we could write and tell her, Mum. You've no need to worry. You will always be my mum. I just feel for Patricia now, knowing what she must have gone through giving me up. I suppose it's because I'm pregnant myself and could just imagine if I was facing that."

Andrew looked to Mary. "Of course we all know what you went through as well. It can't have been easy to accept another baby after losing yours."

"No, it was strange. But I loved her straight away. There was no doubt in my mind that I had done the right thing. It was as though she was a gift from heaven."

Sally wrapped her arms about her mother and together they wept. Andrew also had to pull a handkerchief from his pocket and blow his nose.

45

1952

David and Susannah had sold their house in Hitchin to join their daughter in Vancouver five years after she had gone to make a new life there. Opportunities were more plentiful and David had secured a good job, thanks to Gus's influence and help.

Once they had settled in Susannah had written and asked William and Ellen to join them but they had resisted, saying they were too old to go off gallivanting at their age but wished them well.

Daniel, however was very interested when he heard of the wonderful life they were leading and he asked Alice how she felt about joining them. She agreed immediately. She had missed Susannah far more than she thought possible. No mention was made of Donald going with them. His popularity had not increased over the years as he had become older.

Their going, however, gave Donald the opportunity he needed to move in permanently with his grandparents. He needed somewhere to live and they had plenty of room so were unable to refuse him. This meant that he could keep an eye on things and may even give him the opportunity to search the house. Even after all this time he still felt there was something hidden. It had become as obsession with him. A seed had been planted in his mind and it had grown out of all proportion. It was always there - nagging at him.

Although he was working in his grandfather's business he did as little as was humanly possible to get away with.

William had partly handed over the reins to his colleague, Adam Bradshaw and was taking a less active part in running the business. But his health had deteriorated of late and he was having trouble with his joints, arthritis seeming to be getting the best of him. He was quite low in sprits and Ellen was doing her utmost to keep him cheerful, though at times she felt more than ready to give in. She also was starting to feel her age.

At her suggestion they planned to go away for a week or two and made arrangements to travel down to the south coast.

Donald encouraged this idea. It would give him a great opportunity to do a bit of delving.

As soon as they had left he was in their bedroom going through cupboards and wardrobes. He went through every drawer but could find nothing. It took him a long time as he had to make sure he replaced everything as it had been to avoid any suspicion.

Next he tackled the other bedrooms that were not in use, his mood becoming ever blacker as nothing came to light.

Every waking hour, when he was not at work was spent searching. He went around the house searching for loose floorboards and had found one in the back bedroom. When in the act of lifting it he heard voices in the hall. It was his grandmother speaking. Damn, they had returned earlier then expected - nearly a week, in fact. He hastily replaced the carpet and pulled the chest of drawers back into place. By the time he had got downstairs his grandfather was sitting in the lounge with his grandmother hovering over him.

"You sit there, dear. I'll get you a cup of tea."

"I'd rather have brandy."

When later, Ellen went into her bedroom, she felt the stirrings of unease. Something did not feel right. She looked around the room thinking that perhaps she was imagining it but then noticed that the cheval mirror was not in its usual place. She normally caught her reflection when walking into the room but now had to go nearer to the bed. It had definitely been moved. But why, she could not think. A reflection caught her eye. In the mirror she could see Donald bending over her dressing table, but when she looked round there was no-one there. The mirror was trying to tell her something, she was sure.

William began to deteriorate after their trip. They had returned early as he been in constant pain and wanted to be in his own bed at night.

He was so relieved to be home and had a good night's sleep. The next day he was determined not to lie in bed although Ellen did her best to persuade him. So she made him comfortable in the armchair, his newspaper by his side along with a glass of cider, which was his favourite drink.

The newspaper was forsaken for the present as he sat with his eyes closed and reminisced on the past. He had had a good life and accomplished everything he had set out to do. His marriage had been happy and he was still, even after all this time, very much in love with his dear Ellen. Perhaps the only disappointment had been his son and grandson. They had never shown his enthusiasm for the business as he had hoped.

Oh, they had worked there alongside him when necessary but he had always felt as though their hearts weren't in it. He knew he could not rely on Donald to run it so now that Daniel had upped and gone to Canada he knew he must sell.

It was a sad and traumatic day when he, at last, had let go of the reins and shown the new owner into the office and around the premises. He stayed on for two weeks to show him the ropes and that was even harder for he had had to accept the knowledge that it would all change. Even whilst he was still there machinery and printing presses were being replaced by new modern ones. He knew in his heart that this was good practice but it didn't make it any easier.

Now he must let it all go and concentrate on the present. This damned arthritis didn't help. It made him immobile and was causing him to put on weight. The doctor had warned him about his heart taking too much strain. He hadn't told Ellen this. He didn't want her to worry about him.

His mind, for some reason, often strayed to his friend, Bernard. He had had such a short life and his last years had been torment. Such a waste.

The diamonds still lay where he had hidden them and as they did not need the money he was reluctant to sell them. The money would only end up in Donald's hands and that was something he did not want. He had never shown any initiative to stand on his own two feet. He would always go for the easy option and take whatever he could from life without having to put any effort into it.

46

It was a wet and blustery day when Sally started her labour pains. She just thought she had been doing too much and was suffering from back-ache. But as the day wore on she knew that it was something more serious. The baby wasn't due for another ten days but everything had been ready for a long time.

The week before, a line full of snowy white nappies had been blowing in the wind and the cradle was made up with its flannelette sheet and little lemon cover. As she was to have the baby at home she had gone over the list of requirements and everything was there. Even the sheets of waterproof paper were folded in the corner of the room. When the pains got stronger she stripped the bed and put these in place. This done she went down to the office to telephone the midwife. The ache in her back was now moving round to the front and causing her to catch her breath.

Joe was due home in a couple of hours so she wouldn't call him at work. Perhaps she could pass the time by preparing a meal. She had only got as far as peeling the potatoes when she suddenly doubled up in pain. For a few moments she was unable to move and just bent double over the sink.

Nurse Audrey Carter, the midwife, arrived within half an hour of her being called. Sally was promptly put to bed and Joe arrived as she was being given her first dose of gas and air. She was in a haze of pain and euphoria. Joe, as instructed by the midwife, gently lifted the gas and air mask off her face at times so that she didn't get too much. She was gripping his hand so hard it was almost numb.

An hour later a baby girl lay in Sally's arms and as Sally looked down on her she knew it had been worth every second of pain. She felt there had never been such a beautiful baby ever.

Joe watched entranced as their daughter was washed, then dressed in a white nightdress and matinee jacket. She was then put to the breast and her tiny hand was clasping Sally's finger as she sucked and drank her fill. He then tore himself away to go to the office to telephone Mary and tell her she was a grandmother. He heard the catch in her voice as she answered.

"I'll be there tomorrow afternoon. Give her my love, Joe."

After the midwife had done all she needed and left them Joe lay on the bed beside Sally and his daughter. His heart was so full he felt he would burst. He could only wonder as to how such a tiny being could captivate him so.

Patricia was in Sally's thoughts from morning till night. She couldn't get her our of her mind. Imagine giving this tiny being away. She would rather lose an arm.

She knew she must get in touch with Patricia to tell her of the birth. Then she wondered if perhaps that would be cruel. Would it bring back all the pain? She needed to talk it over with her mother.

As she lay between waking and sleeping her eyes drifted to the cheval mirror. It was wreathed in mist and through it she caught a glimpse of lady in a blue dress. She felt no fear, but only a lovely sense of peace. The lady was smiling. Sally knew then the name she would give to her daughter - Ellen Mary.

47

1955

Williams health continued to deteriorate and by late autumn he was unable to get up from his bed. Ellen employed a live-in nurse to help though she spent every possible hour with him. With someone to do the heavy work it gave her more time to sit and talk. She would read his favourite books to him and get more from the Library.

Adam Bradshaw was a regular visitor to the house and would also sit with William, telling of the latest developments at the printing works. He tried to play down the fact that the latest machinery was a great asset. He knew William did not want things to change and also knew that there was no chance of a visit to the works so he just decided not to say more than he had to.

Adam's visits gave Ellen the chance to wander down to the town or work in the garden. She still found pleasure with her plants. She even enjoyed weeding. She sometimes felt a little guilty as when she was engrossed in her garden she could forget for a while that she would soon lose her loving husband and companion.

Reluctantly Donald helped out with the heavy work such as clearing dead wood and mowing the lawn. Whenever the chance arose he still searched the house but as William's room was out of bounds could do no more in there. Frustration was eating away at his insides.

It was on a blustery day in March when William passed away. Ellen was devastated even though it had been expected. Her husband, friend and soul mate had gone. She had never loved another man. William had been everything she had wanted and theirs had been a perfect marriage.

The funeral was delayed so that Daniel, Susannah and Patricia could fly over from Canada with theirs partners. Many tears were shed during the next few days and they tried to persuade Ellen to return with them but she thanked them and declined their offer. There was no way she could leave her beloved house and even though William was buried in the cemetery she still felt him there beside her and knew she could not leave him either. She kept these thoughts to herself.

So she hugged her loved ones and clung to Patricia, not wanting to let her go when they left in a taxi that was to take them to the airport.

When at last she sat alone in her bedroom she put her head in her hands and sobbed.

The mirror watched.

48

Donald almost rubbed his hands together in glee as he saw how his grandmother deteriorated after the funeral. She had seemed to age considerably and he lived in hope that she would soon follow his grandfather to the grave. She had lost all her sparkle and spent the days sitting in her chair before the fire. She wrote numerous letters to her loved ones in Canada and longed for them to be with her. She hid the fact from them that she was so unhappy and pretended she was filling her life with friendships.

Only Andrew seemed to see the real side of her and knew how she was suffering. He could read her like a book and she was unable to pull the wool over his eyes. Because of this he took to visiting her as often as his workload allowed.

It was on one of these visits that he told her of a position that was going at the hospital. Someone was needed to run a small coffee shop there for a couple of days a week. The true fact, had she but known it, was that he had approached a friend of his and put the idea to him that a coffee shop would be a good idea.

At first she rejected the idea of working there but with a bit of persuasion soon came around to it. It gave her a new lease of life. She helped to set up the shop, which proved a great success. She chatted to customers, met new friends and helped other people to cope with their grief. This lessened the time thinking about her own.

As the weeks went by she took on new challenges, helping out at various charity events and even made friends who took her out and about. The years seemed to drop away from her as she became an independent person.

Andrew Underwood was amazed at the change in her when he visited.

"I can't believe how well you look, my dear."

"I feel it, Andrew. When I lost dear William I never expected to smile ever again. The doctor has told me that I should slow down a bit as my heart is playing up but I told him I have no intentions of sitting around waiting to die. Losing William has taught me one thing and that is we must make the most of every moment. As you well know, he was always so engrossed in the business and that meant we didn't take holidays as we should have done. He always thought the printing works couldn't run without him. And now look. It is managing perfectly well."

"You're right my dear, I suppose we are all guilty of thinking that we are indispensable. Perhaps it is a form of pride when we think people can't do without us. Well, just you take care and don't overdo it"

Donald was quietly seething inside whilst trying to appear caring to his grandmother, though as she had become more independent there was little for him to do. He could do nothing but wait. Money was tight now as she had no intention of indulging him. It often worried her just how much she had come to dislike this grandson of hers. There was something creepy about him. He reminded her of an unpleasant character from a Charles Dickens story. She would catch him creeping around the house, when he thought she wasn't looking, in a sly manner. He brought to mind a spider waiting to catch a fly. She still shuddered at the thought of spiders. If she came across one she would have to ask Donald to remove it for her. He would see her face turn a deathly white as he did so.

An idea began to form in his mind. At the present it was only a tiny thought but as the weeks passed and desperation set in it eventually became as obsession.

***

The winter of 1963 had been long and hard. For many days Ellen had been unable to get to the hospital because of the snow and found herself getting very depressed being shut up with only Donald for company and when she suffered a bad bout of flu she became weak and unable to pick up even when it had passed.

She had never felt so vulnerable in her life. Being a strong woman she had resolved problems for others and even though she faced the distance between herself and her loved ones she had always felt them near. Now she was completely alone and she was frightened.

She felt that if she could get out in the fresh air it would help but Donald kept her cosseted in the warm room often lighting a fire in the grate when it was not needed. She felt as if she was suffocating. Friends stopped calling when told by Donald that she was not up to visitors.

Then came the day when something happened. She thanked God when Donald cut his hand badly on a tin and had to go to the doctor to have it stitched. When he had left the house she struggled out of bed and made her way down to the office to telephone Andrew. He heard the distress in her voice and promised to come within the hour.

By the time he had reached the house Donald was back and did his best to keep him from seeing her, but Andrew persisted and was shown to her bedroom where she lay propped up in bed. He could not help but see the difference in her since they had last met. The weight seemed to have fallen away and her once luxurious hair was lank and unkempt.

He waited for Donald to leave them alone and immediately took her limp hand in his.

"My, dear, whatever is the matter?"

She spoke in such a low voice he had difficulty in hearing her and had to move his ear closer to her.

"I am frightened, Andrew. I can't really tell you why, but I just feel afraid. Donald is so strange. He hovers around me, watching my every move. I know it sounds silly but I feel he is waiting for me to die. The only reason I was able to call you was because he had to go to the doctor. He never leaves my side, except when I'm asleep. I want you to do something for me."

"Anything, me dear."

"Get some paper out of the top drawer in my dressing table and write what I tell you. Then I will sign it."

He did as he was asked and she dictated that should anything happen to her she wanted Donald to be removed from the house immediately. She shakily signed the document and then lay back as if a whole weight had been lifted from her shoulders. She looked peaceful as she closed her eyes.

Andrew sat with her for another hour, albeit with many trivial interruptions from Donald on any pretext he could come up with and when it was time to say goodbye Andrew felt an unease. He truly loved this dear lady whom he had known for so many years and felt helpless to do anything for her.

He made straight for his office and put Ellen's letter in safe keeping. There was some consolation in the fact that Donald should not benefit from anything happening to her.

Only Andrew knew the contents of her will. Donald had no idea that he would be getting nothing when his grandmother died but as he was unaware of this it did not help to allay Andrew's fears for her. He decided he would visit her again as soon as he was able and keep an eye on her. This he did on many an occasion but she never really seemed to pick up. She did manage to sit out in the garden with him a few times and these were the only incidences when she brightened up.

The last time he visited was in late June and the garden was a picture with the roses in bloom. He thought that perhaps, at last, she was on the road to recovery and felt much more optimistic as he left.

He did not know at that moment that he wasn't to see her again.

49

After Donald had seen Andrew off the premises, he knew he had to act. He had felt Andrew watching him. What had the old lady said? Had she told him of her suspicions? He knew his grandmother was a wily old soul and would not let him get the better of her.

"Well, we'll see about that." he spoke the words our loud to himself.

It took him just three days to complete his plan of action. He had done everything he had needed to do. Now he just had to see her off this mortal plane. With a little help, of course.

Ellen sat propped up against her pillows reading. She found it hard to concentrate on the story and her mind kept wandering. For some reason her granddaughter came into her mind. Oh, how she longed to see her. She then thought of Sally and felt a great sense of relief that she had settled her affairs with Andrew, knowing that when she died Sally would get this house. She prayed that she would come to live here. And be as happy as she herself had been.

A movement in the mirror caught her eye and she saw her beloved William there. He was smiling at her. She blinked at the reflection and was amazed to see it still there. So often it disappeared as quickly as it had come. She smiled back at him and felt a warmth envelope her. For the first time in months she no longer felt alone. She drifted off into a calm sleep.

When she was woken by the door opening she started. Donald was entering the room carrying a tray. She must have slept longer than she thought, though she didn't feel hungry and would easily have foregone lunch. The warmth she had felt before she slept had gone from the room and there was a chill in the air. She shivered slightly and pulled her bed-jacket around her. The tray Donald was carrying had a silver salver on it with a lid and as he placed it across her lap he smiled a smile that did not reach his eyes. They were cold.

"There you are, Grandmother. I have a special treat for you."

He placed the tray across her lap and as he lifted the lid the scream that emitted from Ellen's mouth was piercing. Her eyes widened in horror. They were scurrying everywhere - dozens of them. Their black legs running in all directions over her coverlet and onto her nightdress. Some had reached her bare flesh. The scream became a gasp as she struggled for air. She clutched at her throat and her heart pounded in her chest. She could not breathe. Her head felt as though it was going to burst. Her hands moved to her chest and then the blackness began to engulf her as she sunk into oblivion. On her last breath she felt William's hand in hers.

Donald smiled as the eight-legged killers innocently scurried away completely unaware of the anguish they had just caused.

The mirror watched.

50

April 1965

The day that Trip came into their lives was one that Sally would never forget. Joe arrived home with a squirming black bundle in his arms, which, at that time, did not have a name. And when he announced, all in one breath in case Sally interrupted, that a pal of his at work, the same pal, incidentally, who has given him the chickens, had got a litter of puppies and that this one was the one no-one wanted and homes had been found for all the others, Sally laughed and shook her head slowly from side to side.

"They must see you coming, Joe. First it's chickens, now a puppy. What are you going to bring home next?"

"Aw, come on Sal. You know the chickens were a good idea."

"Well, yes, I grant you that. They have been a boon. But this, this thing…well, what good will that be? He's so ugly. His ears are too big for his face."

Joe quickly covered the puppy's ears as he lowered him to the floor.

"Don't say things like that. You'll hurt his feelings. Anyway, he'll grow into them soon. He's ever so affectionate." he said as the puppy jumped up and a long tongue came out trying to lick his face.

"I can see that. Oh, but Joe. He'll be hard work and I have our baby to look after. She takes up all of my time."

"No, honestly, Sal. You won't have to do a thing. I'll take full responsibility for him."

"Oh, yes, and what about when you're at work? No, you'll have to take him back. We definitely can't keep him"

Joe looked contrite.

"OK, if that's how you feel. He'll have to stay with us until Monday though, because Mac's gone away for the weekend."

As Joe was well aware would happen, by the time Monday came, Trip had stolen their hearts and acquired his name - because all he seemed to do was dart through their legs and trip them up.

Joe offered to take him back to Mac, knowing that Sally would not let this bundle of fur on legs go anywhere. She had been completely captivated and his ugliness had grown on her. He had a way of perching himself at her feet and gazing up at her with his jet black eyes. They were hard to see amongst his thick, black fur which had a way of curling, especially when he got a bit hot and damp.

The feelings were mutual because Trip fell head over heels in love with Sally. He thought this being was beautiful and would watch her continually. He saw her tenderness towards the baby and took this feeling on board himself. He felt it was his loyal duty to protect this tiny replica of his mistress. When Ellen was lying on a rug or sitting propped up playing with her toys he would lie with his head on his big paws and gaze at her with soulful eyes.

So the days passed in idyllic hours spent in each other's company. Trip grew at an alarming pace and by the time he was four months old he came up to the rim of the pram and was able to stretch and look in at his charge. Ellen would gurgle at him and chuckle when he softly barked at her. They seemed to have a language all of their own.

***

Donald Bancroft was running out of money and also ideas on how he could get more. He had been threatened by the man he owed debts to, in the form of a severe beating. He had had to stay out of sight for nearly a week whilst his wounds healed. But, more than the pain, he felt an anger against Sally and her good fortune. He still had no idea why she was living in the house instead of himself but knew he had to take drastic measures to put thing right - at least in his eyes.

He knew that if anything should befall her then the house now would go straight to Joe so anything he had thought to do to her was out of the question. But if something happened to Joe perhaps she would leave Hitchin and go to live with her mother. Then he, Donald, could step in and take over. There was no-one else.

He had been stealthily watching Joe and was getting to know all his movements. He knew he took that dog of theirs out for a walk in Ransom's Rec. every evening at around seven o' clock. He would bide his time and wait for the right evening to make his move.

"Surely you're not going out in this." Sally remarked as Joe was putting on his jacket. "It's a real pea-souper out there. You'll never find your way."

Joe picked up Trip's lead as the dog looked up at him expectantly.

"I can't disappoint him, Sal. Just look at him."

"No, I suppose not. Don't be too long though. I shall worry"

"Worry? Don't be silly. You never worry about me, I'm sure"

Sally kissed him. For some stupid reason she did feel worried.

As Joe walked from the front garden and along the road he did not know he was being watched and followed. He kept Trip on the lead as they made there way down Dacre Road and crossed over to the recreation ground. It was normally a busy place with boys playing football and girls standing around making eyes at them. There were swings and a long slide which was nearly always occupied. Tonight though there was an eerie stillness over the whole area. The fog had thickened even more and Joe could hardly see his hand in front of this face. The gloom enshrouded him like a cloak.

"Come on, Trip. Get a move on. Stop sniffing at everything you see. We'll get caught in this fog if we're not careful and then I'll probably lose you altogether."

Trip ignored him completely and continued to smell every root and tuft of grass. He loved this place. The odours that reached his nostrils were delicious. He didn't need his eyes to know that his friend Sukey was just over there. He'll go over to see her and have another sniff.
He bounded off before Joe could stop him.

As Joe strained his eyes to get a glimpse of Trip he heard a sound in the undergrowth. Thinking it was the dog, he turned and as he did so there appeared a figure in front of him. He was wearing a balaclava and only his eyes could be made out in the yellow gloom of the fog. Just then Joe felt a sharp pain in his side. The figure disappeared in the mist and Joe slumped to the ground his fingers wet with his blood as it seeped onto the grass.

Trip had parted from Sukey after satisfying his smelling instincts and was making his way back to Joe when he suddenly got a sense that something was wrong. His animal radar kicked in and told him his master was in danger and his feet hardly touched the ground as he tore across the grass. He came to an abrupt stop when he saw the body of his beloved master and he let out a whelp of anguish and started to lick his face. Getting no response from the still figure he started to bark, each bark terminating in a howl. It was an ear piercing sound that carried through the fog like wildfire. Thankfully it was heard by Sukey's master, Tom Hammond, who was on the scene in a flash.

Tom and Joe had exchanged the odd word or two when the dogs had become friends and although, when Tom peered closer, he recognised the man who lay on the ground he had no idea as to his identity. They had not even exchanged names - only of the dogs.

When he turned Joe over his hand came into contact with a warm, sticky substance. He knew instinctively that it was blood. He told Sukey to stay and ran to his house which was on the outskirts of the recreation ground. After asking his wife to call 999 he went back to the Joe, who by this time had lost a lot of blood. He had grabbed a towel when leaving the house and this he held pressed to the wound to try to stop the flow.

When Joe was being lifted on to the stretcher Trip was beside himself in distress and barked unceasingly. It was as Tom took hold of him to restrain him that he noticed the disc on the dogs collar. By the light of the ambulance he read the name and address. Taking the leads of both dogs he made his way to Joe's home to inform Sally of what had happened.

Sally nearly didn't answer the door when the bell rang. She still had visions of Donald trying to inveigle his way in. It wasn't until Tom called out telling her who he was that she opened the door. He quickly told her what had happened and had to catch her as she nearly passed out. He led her to a chair and offered to make her a cup of tea. He put three spoonfuls of sugar in it as he had heard that was good for shock and when she had taken a few sips Sally immediately telephoned her mother and had difficulty in getting the words out.

"Oh, Mum I don't know what to do. They've taken him to hospital but I don't know how bad he is."

Mary tried to calm her.

"Go round to your neighbour, dear. I'm sure she will help. Perhaps she'll look after Ellen so that you can go to the hospital. I'll leave first thing in the morning. I should be with you by lunch time. Try not to worry, dear. He's in safe hands."

Tom stayed with her until her neighbour came round and then offered to drive her to the hospital.

"Though I must admit I don't know if we'll be able to see where we are going. It's pretty grim out there. I could take Sukey home and walk with you if you would like me to."

"I would like that, please. But you can leave Sukey here if you like. She can keep Trip company. Hadn't you better phone your wife, She'll be worried."

"Thanks. I will, if you'll point me to the phone."

Sally clung onto his arm as they made their way to the hospital. It did not occur to her that she had only just met this man for she was so glad to have someone to lean on. It took them about twenty minutes to reach the hospital in the fog and Sally was shown into the matron's office to be told that Joe was in a bad way. He was in the operating theatre and they were doing all they could for him, but it would be touch and go.

For Joe it was touch and go - for two long days and two long nights Sally spent every moment that she could by his bed and prayed. He had lost a lot of blood by the time they had got him to hospital and he had various tubes going into his body. The knife had punctured his lung and it had taken two hours of surgery to repair the damage. He looked a sorry sight and Sally's love poured out to him. She would die if anything happened to Joe.

The police had not caught the person responsible and it didn't look as thought they ever would. There seemed to be no motive, nothing being stolen and it was a dead end. There was only one man who had his suspicions but he kept them to himself. Andrew didn't want to alarm Sally or give her more worries than she already had.

It was said afterwards that Trip had definitely saved his master's life. He was hailed as a hero and even got a mention with his photo in the local newspaper.

51

It took Joe a long time to get over his attack, not only the physical injuries but to his self-confidence. He no longer walked Trip in the dark on his own, but had become very good pals with Tom and they would walk together. It was a friendship that would last many years. The dogs were thrilled as it meant they could always romp together.

When Donald was attacked one evening it was assumed that there was a link. Little did anyone know that the link was that Donald was getting a taste of his own medicine. His creditors were giving him a warning that if he didn't soon pay up there would be more to come.

Mary stayed with Sally for two weeks and at the end of her visit suggested she and Joe should come to stay with her and Jack for a short holiday.

It was arranged for a week's time before Joe returned to work.

***

Donald had called at the house on the pretext of asking after Joe and offering his help in any way it was needed. Joe thanked him but told him they were going to visit Sally's mother for a week.

This was just what Donald wanted to hear. Unbeknown to anyone he still possessed a key to the house and set to making his plans. A week would be ample time to search the house from top to bottom.

He watched from the wooded area across the road, well hidden by the trees, whilst Joe and Sally climbed into Andrew Underwood's car. He had offered to drive them to the station.

"We really must see about getting a car, Joe, when we get back. I know we don't need one very often but times like this makes me think how nice it would be not to have to rely on other people."

Andrew heard her and spoke in his kindly way. "Now don't you worry, my dear. You know I love to help."

This was the first time since their meeting with Andrew that Joe had been in the car again and he was relishing the trip, albeit only a five minute one. Had it not been for all the inevitable baby necessities besides their own luggage, they probably would have walked but it didn't take much for Joe to find an excuse to go in Andrew's car.

Donald watched them go. He wouldn't make a move until tonight. He wanted to make sure they were well out of the way. He returned to his flat where he poured himself a couple of stiff drinks.

It was after midnight when he finally made his way to the house and slipped in through the gate, closing it quietly behind him. The key he still had in his possession was one to the side door. He tried the high wooden gate leading to the garden. Luckily Joe had not locked it, otherwise it would have been difficult to gain access.

He inserted the key into the lock and turned it and as he let himself into the house he breathed a deep sigh of relief. He had done it - and he had all the time in the world to go about his search. This time he would find what he was looking for, though he still did not know what it was, he reminded himself.

After two hours of searching he was still no nearer to reaching his goal. He was systematically working his way through the house and had covered the first floor bedrooms. It was when he was in Sally and Joe's room that he remembered the mirror and turning towards it recoiled in horror. There was his grandmother smiling at him and slowly shaking her head from side to side.

He stood paralysed to the spot as his hair stood on end. He felt as though he was suffocating. He could not get his breath. He had to get out.

Running down the stairs he made straight for the side door to let himself out into the fresh air - but the door would not open. It was jammed. He made his way to the front door that also remained stuck. It was as though it had been nailed shut. The back door into the garden was the same.

Panic was choking him. He heard laughter. It was his grandmother's voice that he heard. She was laughing at him.

His mind was in a turmoil. There must be some way to get out. Then he had a thought. He remembered when he was small climbing up through the coal chute, much to his cousin's consternation. She was shouting at him not to attempt it. Actually when he started to climb he himself realised how stupid it was but no way was he going to let Patricia know he was scared. As she watched in horror he slowly made his way up and struggling to lift the grating emerged into the fresh air - filthy, but triumphant. He really had no wish to attempt it again but knew he had to get out of this house.

Hurriedly making his way down the lower stairs he could hear his grandmother laughing. His skin crawled. When at the bottom in the inner hallway he lifted the latch let himself into the dark recess and down the stone steps to the cellar. As he descended them he heard a sound as the door closed behind him. There was an eerie silence that was then broken by a soft sigh. He was not alone. There was someone else in here with him. He tried to look around but the darkness prevented him seeing anything. He stumbled back up the steps and tried the door. It would not open. He hammered on it and shouted but there was no-one to hear him. Again he heard the sound of soft laughter.

He was overcome with panic. For the first time for as long as he could remember, he screamed. The darkness closed in on him but although he was unable to see he could still feel and it was then that he felt them - crawling all over him, their black legs running and scurrying all over his body. His screams went unheard. He was entirely alone - or was he? Again came the sound of soft laughter.

52

Because of their long journey to Yorkshire Joe and Sally had left Trip in the care of their neighbour, Tony. They had also asked him to look in on the house occasionally to check everything was OK. It was on the second day they had been away that he let Trip in through the front door and the moment they entered the hallway the dogs hackles rose and he stood motionless and sniffed the air. Tony could sense the dog's discomfort but could not think why this should be. He waited for the animal to move and slowly followed him as he made his way downstairs. When they reached the cellar door Trip stopped and let a piercing howl which made Tony's hair stand on end.

He gently lifted the latch and opened the door. Trip excitedly ran down the steps and started barking.

It was not until Tony had returned to his own house and poured himself a stiff drink that he was able to tell his wife what he had found. The police were called and the body moved.

"I suppose we must telephone Joe and Sally but I hate to spoil their holiday. Joe needs it so much. This on top of everything else will be the end of him. What do you think we should do?"

"How about we get someone else to phone - someone whose voice they don't know. Then we could ask for Jack or Mary and explain to them. It's not the sort of thing you can say on the phone"

"That's a good idea."

It was agreed by Jack and Mary to keep the information of Donald's death from Sally and Joe until they got home and this arrangement had the full co-operation of the local police. It was confirmed that Joe could have had nothing to do with the death because of the time.

It was a mystery as to why Donald should have been at the house, how he had entered and what he was doing in the cellar. It was an even larger mystery as to the cause of death. It was as if he had been blown out like a candle - his life had been extinguished with no visible cause.

When Andrew Underwood heard of the death he couldn't help feeling a sense of relief. He had never trusted him and now felt that a cloud had been lifted from Sally's life. He would play down the incident as much as possible. The last thing he wanted was for Sally's love of the house to be tainted.

He immediately telephoned Daniel in Canada who talked it over with his family and it was agreed that they should all come to England for the funeral. Except Susannah, who was suffering from a bad bout of bronchitis and had been advised by her doctor it would be most unwise to fly. Andrew booked them into The Lister Hotel and it was four days later when they arrived.

Joe and Sally got home to find Andrew waiting on the doorstep and as they entered the house he ushered them into the lounge where he told them what had happened. He also told them that Daniel, Alice, Patricia and Gus were in town and Sally knew she had to make a decision whether to see her natural mother or not.

She telephoned Mary and although she knew it would be painful Mary did not hesitate in suggesting Sally invited them to the house. She would travel down to support her.

So it was the day after the funeral that Andrew arranged for them to visit.

Mary had written to tell Patricia of Ellen's birth and had received an answer to the effect that she was happy for Sally but felt she had no place in her life and should keep her distance. Now that was all changed because of the circumstances of Donald's death. Here they were on the doorstep. Mary let them in and showed them through to the dining room.

To Patricia it felt so strange being in the house again. The house where she had spent so many happy times with her grandmother. It had changed very little and she almost feel her grandmother there still, expecting her to walk through the door at any moment. Tears welled up in her eyes when the thought came to her that she would never see that dear face again.

The door opened and Sally came through carrying a squirming little girl in her arms. She was reluctant to put her down and held her as a shield between herself and the person standing in front of her. It was like looking at an older version of herself. She knew without any doubt that this was her natural mother.

Both stood in silence as though turned to stone. Neither knew how to act. Then as if the years had rolled away Patricia took her into her arms and held her. She was her baby again. This being whom she loved so much and had thought about every day of her life.

Mary watched as the two held each other and was surprised to feel no animosity towards Patricia. She had given Mary a precious gift many years ago and now she must return it to her - maybe for only a few moments - or maybe for much longer. Who could tell?

Gus stood in the background through these exchanges. Patricia had not told him of Sally's existence until they were about to leave home to travel to England and he still couldn't quite take it in. He was finding it very hard to relate to the fact that this attractive girl was his daughter. But then, he had not carried her inside him for ninth months, nor held her to the breast and cuddled her as Patricia had done. He felt a little guilty that he did not instantly love her. But then, he reasoned, she was a stranger. Someone he had just met. The one thing that did move him was the likeness to his dear wife. He loved Patricia with every fibre of his being and it gave him joy to see her so happy meeting her daughter again after all this time.

Patricia and Sally spent two wonderful days in each other's company and Patricia spent many hours at the house and had asked Sally if she could explore it again to re-capture her childhood.

"Of course you can. Take as long as you like. I love this house and feel so privileged that your grandmother left it to me. I often feel her here, you know. She must have been a lovely lady."

"Oh, she was. She was the sweetest person in the whole world."

Then Sally remembered the dresses that were hanging in her wardrobe.

"There's something I want to show you. Come up to my bedroom."

When Sally opened the wardrobe door and pulled out the dresses to lay them on the bed Patricia gasped.

"Oh, I didn't know Grandmother had kept these."

She reverently fingered the dress of cream lace.

"This must be my mother's wedding dress. Oh, and I remember grandmother wearing this green silk one when I was little."

She held it to her nose and breathed in deeply.

"I can still smell her perfume."

Tears welled up in her eyes and spilled onto her cheeks.

Sally said softly "Would you like to have them? They really belong to you more than me."

"Oh, I would love them. Thank you Sally. I will treasure them. My mother will be thrilled to see it again"

"Have you any idea what Donald was looking for in the house? He has been pestering us for months - ever since we moved in. I've always been a little scared of him. And then for him to die in the cellar - well there must have been something he was searching for. Do you know if there is anything valuable here?"

"Not that I know of. Gran and Grandfather were comfortably off but never rich. And if they had anything of value surely my mother would have known. No, I really don't know what he was doing here. He always was a nasty piece of work though. I know we shouldn't speak ill of the dead but I went through some horrible times with him when I was little. He never seemed to keep any friends and always tried to turn mine against me. I think he was jealous because I had so many. I shouldn't worry. Don't let it spoil your love of the house."

At that moment a sound was heard behind them and as they turned as one they caught sight of a face in the mirror. It was a beautiful lady with her dark auburn hair swept up in a chignon. She was smiling at them both. They automatically smiled back without a second thought. Then, after the initial shock, they looked at each other and burst out laughing. When they looked back the figure had gone.

There was one more surprise for Patricia and that was a visit from two very special people. Sally had telephoned them to ask if they could visit and they had not hesitated in saying yes.

When Johnny and Betty walked into the room she could not believe her eyes. They were both attractive adults but she would have known Johnny anywhere, with his blonde hair still tumbling over his eyes. Betty perhaps was not quite so recognisable. She was a young lady of fashion in her Mary Quant outfit.

They hugged and held each other and were still talking two hours later when it was time for them to leave.

"We'll never forget what Aunt Ellen did for us. Without her we would not be where we are now."

"I can assure you that what she did for you was returned ten-fold. She loved having you. I think it was you who helped her get through the war. She was always writing and telling me of your antics especially the incident of the damsons."

They all laughed as the tale was told to Sally and Joe.

"Do you still play the trumpet?"

"Oh, yes. It's the only thing I do now. I'm in a band. That's how I came to know Sally. I was here to do a concert."

Betty spoke and praised her brother.

"He's one of the best."

She then asked if she could go round the house and when Sally told her to do so she wandered from room to room and re-lived her childhood memories.

When they eventually climbed into Johnny's smart red car and drove away Patricia waved until they were way out of sight. She had invited them to come and stay with her in Vancouver and Johnny had said they would in a couple of months time.

When the time came for them to part and for Patricia to make her way back to Canada with Sally's father they hugged and held each other. Patricia felt as thought she never wanted to let her go.

Joe and Sally had promised that when Ellen was a little older they would visit Canada for a holiday and get to know them better.

After they had left to return home Sally took her adopted mother in her arms and held her.

"Thank you, Mum, for being so understanding. There will never be anyone to take your place."

Mary broke down and sobbed as her daughter said those words.

Andrew proved to be a rock during the next few weeks, helping them to cope with the inquest and subsequent newspaper interest. It would remain a mystery for a long time to come as to why Donald had been in their cellar. Sally still thought that he had been searching for something, but what she couldn't fathom. Would she ever know?

53

It had been raining non-stop for three whole days and when water began to leak through the roof Joe was aghast. He immediately got a roofer to look into it and was flabbergasted when he got a quote. It was astronomical - way above anything he could afford, and yet it was a problem that would not go away. It could only get worse. And get worse it did. The next torrential rain they had meant them having to situate buckets and bowls in various places on the top floor.

For the first time since their move into the house they began to realise just how much it cost to keep in good repair. The money Sally had received from Ellen had long since dried up and Joe's wage was enough for them to live on but left no extra to spend on any major repair.

"Well, if we can't get it done we will have to consider selling up."

As Joe said this, Sally's heart gave a lurch. She could not imagine leaving this lovely house. She was hoping that Joe could come up with an answer and put the suggestion into oblivion. But he could not. He knew how Sally felt about this place but no way could they come up with the cost of a new roof - albeit only a section of it.

They thought of asking Jack and Mary but knew they would not be able to help, though they would struggle to do so if they possibly could. It wouldn't be fair on them to put them in that position.

Andrew had at last succumbed to his son's persuasion of the offer to stay with him and had decided to take two months off work to go out to Canada to visit. He was long past retirement age but was unwilling to let go of the reins. He appreciated now just how William had felt when he had had to do so.

However, he agreed to take a break. He would accept his son's offer of a holiday and go from there. Perhaps he would feel more ready for retirement when he got back.

He visited Sally to say goodbye and she was thrilled for him. She knew how lonely he was and "You never know" she told him, "perhaps you may like it out there and decide to stay." Though as she said this she couldn't help but have a catch in her throat. This dear man had come to mean so much to her. She couldn't imagine not having him around. He had become a part of her life

She didn't tell him of their worries over the house. There was nothing he could do and it would only worry him. She didn't want to spoil his holiday for the world.

So he set off for Canada and was completely unaware that an estate agent was calling the next day to evaluate the house. Sally made herself scarce when he came. She couldn't bare the thought of someone coldly walking round her beloved house and assessing its worth.

Attaching Trip's lead to his collar she spoke softly to him and nuzzled her nose into his fur.

"Come on, we'll go for a nice walk."

She made her way along Walsworth Road and turned to go up Windmill Hill. It was quite steep and by the time she had reached the top she was out of breath. Seeing a wooden seat she lowered herself onto it and sat gazing down onto the town. She had come to love this town and, as she sat, her thoughts turned to Ellen Bancroft.

"I wonder if you ever sat here. I wish I could have seen it as it was when you were young. It must have been beautiful looking down on Hermitage Road when it was just trees."

Trip ran around on the grass for half an hour or so until Sally called him and they set off up the alley way past The Girl's Grammar School and back down Highbury Road.

When she got home Joe told her of the price the agent had suggested putting the house on the market for. It was a good one and reluctantly they put the sale in his hands. He came back the next day to take numerous photographs and draw up the details.

When these were placed in the newspaper the next week it caught the eye of Harry Jones. He was always on the lookout for a bargain and was scrutinising the pages when seeing the image something tugged at his memory. It was of a night months ago when Donald had partaken of too much whiskey and was pleading with his debtor to wait a little longer.

"Just another month or two - please. I promise I will have the money then. I know how to get it. There'll be far more than I owe you, I'm sure. I only need to find it. I can't tell you anymore about it at the moment but I can guarantee you will be surprised"

He had ranted on about something of value in the house which he only had to find to be rich. Harry Jones had not taken much notice at the time but now he thought about it more deeply.

He had thought at the time that this was just another of Donald's feeble excuses and was considering re-arranging Donald's face to teach him a lesson. But now, when the words Donald had spilled out went over and over in his mind, something about this latest plea caught his imagination. Donald seemed to be sure that there was something of real value hidden in his grandmother's house. The more whiskey Donald had drunk the more loose his tongue had become and now as Harry thought about it he remembered diamonds being mentioned.

Donald's mysterious and untimely death had puzzled him and left him devastated. It was not the death of this man but the fact that it left him being owed more than two thousand pounds.

So perhaps this would be worth looking into. He made for the estate agents office and casually picked up the details along with some other of no interest, whatsoever. He did not want the assistant to think he was too interested. The house was on the market for four thousand pounds, which was a good asking price. If he could raise that amount he could buy the place and tear it apart. He wished now that he had taken more of an interest when Donald had told him about the diamonds but it had passed from his mind quite quickly and he had forgotten it until now.

He had been told there was already other interest in the house so he knew he must move quickly. He would have to cash in a lot of his assets and forcibly call in a few debts, but it could be done.

54

Sally was in the depths of despair. She couldn't eat. She couldn't sleep. They were going to lose their home. It did not help when Joe had said they could buy another place and still have cash over to have a good holiday. They could go to visit Patricia, he told her, and perhaps Mary would come with them.

He tried all ways to try to cheer her up, but she would not be consoled. She would wander from room to room trying to put every nook and cranny in her memory for when she had to leave. She had come to love this house and always felt Ellen's presence especially when she sat in her bedroom.

It was when she was doing this one morning that she heard a rustle. She jumped up in alarm. She was alone in the house and felt the hairs stand up on her head.

When she had been told of the discovery of Donald's body in the cellar she could not bring herself to go down there and yet in some ways she was relieved that he would no longer be visiting. There had been something menacing about him. Now the mystery remained as to what he had been doing here and if he was looking for something what was it?

The rustle got louder and she looked towards the cheval mirror. She did not see her reflection but one of a lady in a blue dress. She knew it was her great grandmother. She was not smiling this time but crying. Tears were streaming down her face and her eyes were appealing to Sally.

Sally felt no fear now. Just a deep sadness for this lovely lady. When she had discovered that she was actually Ellen's great granddaughter she felt a deep love for this person.

If only she could communicate with her. She felt there was something Ellen was trying to tell her.

She sat on the bed and concentrated really hard. The figure was enclosed by a mist and it was hard to make but then the mist started to clear. Ellen was holding a letter in her hand as though she was offering it, but of course it was only a mirage. There was no way Sally could take it from her. Sally had never felt so helpless in her life.

She spoke out loud, feeling rather foolish talking to a mirror.

"Is there a letter, somewhere?"

The reflection answered with a nod of the head and a smile came to the beautiful lips.

"Is it in this house?"

This time there was shake of the head and the smile disappeared.

"Does someone else have the letter?"

This time a nod.

Then Sally had a thought.

"Is it Andrew Underwood?"

This time a repeated nod and a big smile.

Oh, if only she could step into the mirror and hold this lady and let her hug her. She watched as the figure slowly disappeared and all she saw was her own reflection.

That evening she told Joe what had happened and was surprised when he did not laugh at her or make fun of her. He actually believed her.

"What are we supposed to do. Sal? Andrew is away for at least another two weeks and we have already exchanged. We are due to complete in just over two week's time."

They could not believe how quickly the whole transaction had gone through. Harold Jones pushed aside any suggestion of a survey and didn't seem to care whether the roof leaked or not. He just wanted to get in as soon as possible.

"I'll call in the office tomorrow and see if I can get Andrew's son's address. Perhaps his secretary will give me a telephone number. Then I can contact him."

She eventually got the number although Mrs Croft, Andrew's personal secretary, was reluctant to disclose it at first. It was only when Sally got upset and persuaded her how important it was that she relented and gave it to her.

That evening she tried without fail to contact Andrew and many evenings following. She did, however, eventually get an answer a week later from a Mr Hoskins who happened to be there to do some decorating. He told her that Mr Underwood and his son were due home in two days time.

"Please, *please* get him to call me. Tell him it is *so* important."

When Sally eventually got to speak to Andrew and explained what was happening he was appalled that the house was being sold.

"Why didn't you tell me, Sally?"

"I didn't want to spoil your holiday. And I didn't think we would sell it to quickly. It seems that Mr Jones is very keen to get in as soon as possible."

"Mr Jones? What is his first name?"

"Harold, I think."

When Andrew heard the name of the buyer he froze. Harry Jones was renowned in the town for his dodgy dealings and some very serious cases of injuries had been put down to him, but he had always seemed to escape prosecution. The thought of him acquiring Ellen Bancroft's house sent a shiver through him. That's the last thing she would ever have wanted.

She then went on to tell Andrew of the reflection in the mirror.

"There is a letter, Sally. I will get the next available flight home. How long have we got?"

"We complete in four days."

There were just twenty four hours left until the deadline when Andrew knocked on Joe and Sally's door. He was looking the picture of health. Obviously his holiday had done him the world of good.

Sally gave him a hug.

"I'm so sorry to have cut your holiday short."

"Please don't worry, my dear. This is much more important than my holiday. Though I really don't know how it's going to help."

Out of courtesy Sally offered him a cup of tea and was pleased when he declined and said they should get down to business. He opened his brief case and withdrew a manila envelope and when he handed it to her she held it close. She could feel her grandmother's presence and though she was dying to open it there was also a reluctance to do so in case their hopes were shattered.

Andrew explained.

"Ellen gave this to me with instructions that I was to give it to you when you have been living here for three years. I honestly do not know what it says and have no idea whether it will help your present situation but I think now that she would like you to have it."

"And you have no idea what it says?"

Andrew shook his head.

"She was very mysterious about it. I think she was just being cautious. After all, she didn't know how you would take to living in the house. She said she wanted to know you were happy and settled here before she told you something. I trust that is what is in the letter."

Sally carefully slit open the envelope and unfolded the piece of paper. She read it out loud and the others gaped in amazement.

Dear Sally,

When you read this you will have been living in my house for three years. I trust you are as happy here as I have always been.

You will probably have wondered why I entrusted my house to you. You may know the reason now but in case you don't I must tell you. I hope your mother will forgive me but I am hoping you already know that you are my great granddaughter. Please ask your mother to explain if she has not already done so.

Donald has no idea of our relationship and I do not doubt that he will do all in his power to get the house. I hope he has not been a trial to you. I know he will not have taken kindly to your inheritance.

Now, there is something else I want to tell you.

Many years ago, William and I were entrusted with something of great value by a dear friend who suffered badly at the hands of the Nazis. As I write this it is hidden at the top of the house. Please accept it with my love as I know Bernard would have wanted you to.

It is hidden under a floor board outside the box-room. If you lift the loose floor board you will find a brass ring inserted. Lift this and you will find what you are looking for. May it bring you happiness.

Yours affectionately,
your ever-loving great grandmother
Ellen Bancroft.

No-one moved for a full minute. They were all trying to digest the contents of the letter. Then, as one, they all turned and mounted the stairs - Joe and Sally two at a time, Andrew a little slower.

When they had reached the top of the house outside the box-room Sally pulled the lino back and felt for a loose floor board. She found it immediately and lifted it to reveal a small brass ring. The others watched with baited breath as she pulled it. A loose piece of wood lifted to reveal an opening in which was a small box. She lifted it out and on opening it found a black velvet bag. It was soft to the touch and as she held it she heard the sound of a long drawn - out sigh. It was not only her who heard it. Both Andrew and Joe experienced a cold chill down their spine.

Sally pulled at the string which held the bag closed and let the contents spill out onto her hand. There was a small pile of diamonds glinting in the afternoon sunshine that trickled in through the bedroom doorway. She had never held anything like it in her life and thought them beautiful.

"My God" Joe exclaimed. "They must be worth a fortune. Now we know what Donald was looking for. Mind you don't drop any. If they fall between the boards we'll never get them back."

Sally gently let them flow back into the velvet bag and pulled the string tight. Her voice was choked as she turned to her husband and spoke.

"Oh, Joe, you know what this means. We don't have to sell the house and we can get the roof repaired. Ellen didn't want us to go. Oh, thank you Ellen. Thank you, thank you."

Another deep sigh was heard - this time one of satisfaction. It was followed by the sound of soft laughter.

Harold Jones drew up outside the Estate agents and parked his Bentley. Strutting into the office he was surprised to see Joe and Sally waiting for him with smiles on their faces. Surely they should be looking downcast.

Joe spoke first.

"Mr Jones. I'm afraid you have had a wasted journey. The sale is no longer taking place."

The man who faced him went red in the face. He was livid.

"But that can't be. We've made a deal. We've exchanged. You can't go back on a contract."

At this point Andrew stepped forward. He had a huge smile on his face as he spoke.

"There has been no completion, Mr Jones. My clients are quite entitled to cancel the exchange contract. You will receive the normal ten per cent compensation."

"I don't want your bloody ten per cent. I want that house."

"You are not going to get it."

No matter how much he ranted and raved Harold knew he was beaten. He slammed the door as he left and roared off down the road in his large, shiny, black car.

Epilogue

Christmas 1973

The house was full to the brim with people, and laughter seemed to ring out in every room as Sally and Joe mingled with their guests.

The party had been planned for many months, partly to celebrate Christmas but the real reason was to mark ten years in the house that Sally had inherited all those years ago.

Gus and Patricia had come over from Vancouver along with Susannah, David, Daniel and Alice. They were all staying at The Lister Hotel but the house had two special guests who had been given their own bedrooms. They were the same bedrooms they had occupied when they had been evacuees. Only this time Johnny was given the larger room as he had his wife, Tina, with him and his daughter, Jenny.

Betty's husband had been unable to make it because he was on duty as a policeman.

Johnny proudly showed his wife all round the house as though it belonged to him. He felt it did in a way. It would always be in his heart. They wandered from room to room and Tina laughed as he told her of the antics that he and Betty had got up to during their stay.

"Put your coat on, darling. I'll show you the garden."

His daughter who was running around with Ellen and her sister, Sophie, who was a year younger, heard him.

"Can we come too, Dad?"

"Well, it's pretty cold out there. You'd better ask Auntie Sally."

It was ten minutes later when they all had coats and scarves on. Matthew, Sally's youngest, who was just two, was snug in a siren suit of royal blue.

They were all squealing as they ran out of the back door and chased poor Trip down the garden path. He wasn't a youngster anymore but still had a lot of life in him and he adored the children. They could pull his tail, comb his fur and even on occasion dress him up and he still remained calm and happy.

Betty had also joined them outside and as she and Johnny reached the damson tree she burst out laughing.

"I can still see you now, Johnny, lying there with the ladder on top of you and surrounded by damsons."

The story, that had been related so many times, was told once again.

When they all piled back into the scullery to discard boots and coats their cheeks were rosy with the cold and as Sally watched them, she felt such happiness that it brought a lump to her throat.

Patricia and Gus had visited twice since Sally had first met them but she and Joe had yet to get to Vancouver. She had been far too busy having and raising their children but they had promised themselves they *would* get there one day.

Andrew Underwood was not at the re-union. He had at last gone to live with his son in Canada and was happily spending his last years in comfort and companionship enjoying watching his grandchildren in their adult years. He still kept in touch with Sally.

Mary came up behind Sally as she was preparing the fruit punch and put her arms around her waist.

"Happy, darling?"

Mary turned and hugged her.

"Oh, Mum. You'll never know how much. Do you know, I'm sure Ellen is watching over us?"

"I'm sure she is. Have you seen her lately?"

"Just occasionally I catch a glimpse of her in the mirror. And do you know what? She's always smiling."